CONTENTS

Chapter 1 – Victoria.....5
Chapter 2 – Jacob.....17
Chapter 3 – Victoria.....29
Chapter 4 – Jacob.....41
Chapter 5 – Victoria.....56
Chapter 6 – Jacob.....68
Chapter 7 – Victoria.....80
Chapter 8 – Jacob.....90
Chapter 9 – Victoria.....102
Chapter 10 – Jacob.....111
Chapter 11 – Victoria.....123
Chapter 12 – Jacob.....133

Run

LINDA AKSOMITIS

Published by Pearson Education Limited, Edinburgh Gate, Harlow, Essex, CM20 2JE.

www.pearsonschools.co.uk

First published by Pearson New Zealand
a division of Pearson New Zealand Ltd
67 Apollo Drive, Rosedale, North Shore 0632, New Zealand
Associated companies throughout the world

Original edition edited by Lucy Armour
Original edition designed by Sarah Laing and Ruby-Anne Fenning
This edition designed by Sara Rafferty

First published 2007
This edition published 2013

17 16 15 14 13
10 9 8 7 6 5 4 3 2 1

British Library Cataloguing in Publication Data
A catalogue record for this book is available from the British Library

ISBN 978 0 435 14442 5

Printed in Malaysia (CTP-VP)

Acknowledgements
We would like to thank Bangor Central Integrated Primary School, Northern Ireland; Bishop Henderson Church of England Primary School, Somerset; Bletchingdon Parochial Church of England Primary School, Oxfordshire; Brookside Community Primary School, Somerset; Bude Park Primary School, Hull; Cheddington Combined School, Buckinghamshire; Dair House Independent School, Buckinghamshire; Glebe Infant School, Gloucestershire; Henley Green Primary School, Coventry; Lovelace Primary School, Surrey; Our Lady of Peace Junior School, Slough; Tackley Church of England Primary School, Oxfordshire; and Twyford Church of England School, Buckinghamshire for their invaluable help in the development and trialling of the Bug Club resources.

Every effort has been made to contact copyright holders of material reproduced in this book. Any omissions will be rectified in subsequent printings if notice is given to the publishers.

PEARSON

A division of Pearson New Zealand Ltd

CHAPTER 1
Victoria

My stepbrother, Jacob, runs through sunburnt grass and whistles, the trill echoing over the meadow. Mr Higgins' bay stallion lifts his head, whinnies and gallops, black tail rippling, to his outstretched hand.

Jacob shouldn't be there. He should be at my papa's side, in our hardware store, cleaning shelves or pricing yesterday's stock.

I should tell.

Bending, I pull another sheet from the basket and pin it to the clothesline. It catches the wind and fills, like a four-cornered sail that carries my spirit to heaven, to Mama.

Mother Alice calls, "Torrie?"

"Victoria. My name's Victoria," I mutter as the wind gusts and the sheet twists and a tear falls on my cheek.

She steps past the painted door – dull brown hair streaked with grey, lips shut so tight that wrinkles ripple past her cheeks to her rain-cloud eyes.

"Torrie?"

"Coming, Mother Alice," I say and grab the wicker basket, careful not to glance towards the meadow.

I'll keep his secret. For now.

At supper I catch the smell of perfect brown loaves of bread fresh from the oven, lathered with the soft, salty butter she's made.

Mama didn't milk cows or grow a garden or gather wild roots to brew tea. She weighed up bags of nails, counted out saw blades and plough shears, measured out coils of rope and tallied the totals in ink until her hands were stained black.

Papa sits at the table, his blue eyes as deep as the town well that waters us all – people, horses, cattle, sheep and dogs. "Lizzy," he says to my little sister and holds out his hands. "Come sit on Papa's knee."

Elizabeth, not Lizzy, I think, remembering her name on Mama's lips as she rocked to and fro, to and fro – a white swaddled bundle held tight against her breast. Papa's baby girl was always Elizabeth before Mother Alice came to live at our house.

But I smile when Elizabeth drops her rag doll and throws herself against his heart. She has Mama's green eyes and Papa's black curls and everyone's love.

I wonder, what would my baby brother look like if he were here, not wrapped in Mama's lifeless arms?

Jacob dries his hands, pulls a chair over the linoleum floor and flops down, not acting one bit guilty, although I know he left his duties in the store to run, to touch sunshine and the horse's mane.

"Did you see the deer, Victoria?" he asks, his chestnut eyes following the green and black pattern at his feet, not daring to meet mine. "It leapt the fence, racin' round the meadow till it disappeared, while you were hangin' clothes."

He knows I saw him, wonders if I told.

Let him worry.

After the table is cleared, the dishes washed and the electric lights have come on for the night,

I take out a book and quiz Jacob on his letters. Someday I will be a teacher, only my students will be small, not tall, not hating every minute.

I point.

He mutters, "The cat is black."

We talk when we need to, but not in a very friendly way.

I imagine him in my school – shaggy dark hair tickling half-moon, bushy brows over a hawk nose, his limbs sticking out like grasshopper legs from a pea pod body, all spilling out of a desk. Not in my classroom. Not with Margaret and me.

On Saturdays when we played school, Margaret always puckered up her face, like she was eating lemons, and said, "Class, I'm Miss Lowsley, your new teacher. I expect obedience here."

Then we laughed as she waggled her finger at our best china dolls, while I sat them up proper and showed them a slate of A, B, Cs.

The letters blur as I stare, searching for ones Jacob will get, to show Papa I can be a teacher. My fingertip slides across the slippery page and stops.

Chapter One

"The dog made the cat run," Jacob whispers quickly. "That one is *run*," he says again, stretching out each word, until I feel his stride across the meadow of words.

I'm running, too, at least in my head.

Across the room, Papa closes the paper. Mother Alice takes Elizabeth by one hand and Papa rises, takes her other one. Then they go outside to the new garden, all three leaving us behind.

Later, the sounds of town tiptoe through my open window. Next door, the boys argue over who will clean the manure out from the livery stable tomorrow.

"Not me," shouts Sam, his voice cracking on the "e", like it always does.

"Yes, you," replies his brother. "I did it last."

I try to close my eyes and whirl away from 1911 to a time when I've gone away to school, learning to be a teacher, starting over on my own.

Instead, a dull throb moves across my head and I wonder how long it's been there. Maybe since this morning?

I curl up in the narrow iron bed, trying not to touch Elizabeth, almost asleep, her small chest rising and falling. She turns, wraps a chubby arm around me and mutters, "Torrie, I'm tired."

"Me, too," I tell her, moving away from her warmth. "Just go to sleep. I'll be right here beside you, taking care of you."

The night is too hot. My nightgown sticks to my skin, scratching me with invisible fingers that don't leave a mark. Lying very still is the only way to make them stop.

Elizabeth's curls spread out beside me, like the dark vines among the flowers embroidered on the pillowslips that Mama made. I remember thin strands of thread – reds, blues, yellows – dragged through linen held tight between two wooden hoops. As her fingers flew, Mama talked of being home in England, of her sister, Elizabeth, stitching columbine, hollyhock and phlox on Queen Victoria's nightgown, her handiwork the envy of the other ladies-in-waiting.

In the starlight, my sister's china-doll face crinkles with a dreamy smile as she rolls towards the blue striped paper that covers the wall. Watching her, I drift away to a world of restless dreams. Somewhere between full moon and sunrise, my stomach rolls and the mutton stew from supper kicks me in the belly.

The bed sheet that clings to my sweaty body pulls away when I leap from the bed and run, hand over mouth.

Thump. Thump. Thump.

My feet hit hard, the sound echoing through the short corridor between me and the door. Outside, the night smothers me – the air on one side, my body the other, and the sickness between.

When I drop to my knees over the toilet hole, I'm glad for the wooden seat to lean against. The acrid smell fills me, but I'm too sick to care. The last thing I want is Mother Alice holding my shoulders while my stomach empties itself, but she does anyway.

Her hands are strong.

When the heaving stops, I lean back into her arms, let them pull me to my feet. Against my back, the softness of her chest through her threadbare nightgown feels good. She is a mother after all, even if she's not my mother.

Inside the house, the lamp takes the place of the electric lights put out at midnight. Papa and Jacob sit together at the table, eyes staring through me, as Mother Alice half carries, half drags me into the room.

"All right, Victoria?" Papa asks.

Jacob says nothing, just turns away to fill a cup with water.

I don't want to worry Papa, so I nod. "I'm fine. Don't fret," slips past the bitter taste in my mouth.

Papa glances wordlessly at Mother Alice, but I see the question.

She answers, "Doesn't seem like the flu Lizzy had. 'Tis likely just the heat. I shouldn't have kept her in the garden so long this morning. The sun was hot."

It was. My forehead burns against her arm, as if the sun is still upon me. I hate those lessons in the garden: solemn and grim, harder even than Miss Wickham's science class. Why is it that weeds seem stronger, more worthy, than vegetables, clinging to life between clumps of hard dirt?

All the other summers of my life I stayed out of the sun, played games and read with Margaret, or helped Mama in the hardware store. Now I wear a bonnet to keep my face from turning brown in the sun.

"Let Lizzy sleep," says Mother Alice, her voice softening. "Don't want her sick again."

Papa stands, steps across the room, then pushes back the doors to the parlour. The flickering lamp-light casts shadows there –long, secret shadows, dark shadows of memory. I blink, then rub my eyes to make certain that I'm awake.

For a second, the piano played and Mama's coffin filled the parlour – the only room that's still hers, even in death.

Mother Alice gives orders: "Jacob, bring fresh sheets. Edward, get the blanket off the sofa. Those pillows, too – she'll be needin' a plain one for her head." She settles me against the back of Mama's favourite rosewood chair, while Jacob and Papa hurry to their tasks. I close my eyes to keep from spinning after them.

Jacob murmurs something to Mother Alice, then fabric flaps as it did yesterday – was it yesterday? – in the wind and the scent of morning glories fills the room. I hear her smooth the sheet, plump up the pillow, push the short sofa table across the hardwood floor.

With my last bit of strength I stand, smiling weakly. "Papa, I'll be fine. Please go back to bed," I say. "You, too, Jacob," I add, wishing he hadn't heard the commotion I made from his garret room.

Mother Alice nods at them – more an order than a reassurance – as she sets to the business of getting me settled.

The sofa is hard, its horsehair stuffing less yielding than the animal's back it once covered.

Knees bent, I wriggle to fit between arms at either end. Not brown or blonde in the half-light, my hair spreads over the flour-sack pillowcase beneath my head. It's one of Mother Alice's, not Mama's.

I close my eyes and drift away.

Suddenly, a chill starts in my fingers, pulling them tight as it courses through my body. My teeth chatter. My legs quiver. My breath becomes a gasp.

Mother Alice spreads a blanket over me and I wonder why she is still here. Why hasn't she gone to bed? Soon it will be morning. Elizabeth will awaken. Papa and Jacob will want breakfast before they leave for the store.

She should be asleep, but I'm glad she's not, and feel guilty.

The next time I open my eyes, I can see Papa through the sliding doors, sipping his morning cup of tea. Sunshine covers him, covers the table, covers Mother Alice as she wipes one hand across the blue and white checks of her gingham apron, leaving a smear of porridge behind.

"How are you this morning, Victoria?" Papa calls, his voice full of sunshine, too. "All better?"

Around me, the gold in the parlour's wallpaper is swallowed by the dark blue sea it floats in. The window hides behind heavy damask drapes, keeping the walls of family portraits safe from the eyes of passers-by who might stare in. There's no sunshine here at all.

Jacob opens the kitchen door and chases Elizabeth into the room. How did I sleep through her morning noise? He, too, looks my way, then quickly averts his gaze. Not Elizabeth. She skips across the floor until she's caught in Jacob's arms.

I try to sit, to reassure Papa that I am fine. But I'm not. I fall back against the rough texture of the pillow, too weak even to cry.

"Keep Lizzy at the table," says Mother Alice to Jacob, filling two bowls at the black iron stove. She doesn't have to say what she means – we all understand. Keep Elizabeth away from me in the dark room.

Elizabeth clambers up the chair beside Papa, grabs his arm and demands, "Me, too." He reaches for her bowl, sprinkles it with sugar and asks, "Enough?"

She always asks for more.

At the sink, Mother Alice lifts the ladle from the pail, pours water into a cup and hands it to Jacob without a word. He strides across the floor towards me.

Before I can worry about the awkwardness of it all, he has me sitting up, the cup to my mouth, cool water trickling past my fever-cracked lips.

Nothing can be worse than this.

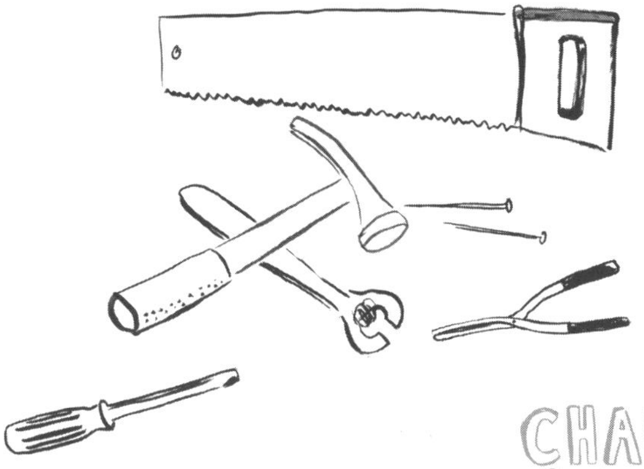

CHAPTER 2
JACOB

The cup I'm holdin' is still half full of water when Victoria's head flops back on the pillow. Now her blue eyes are shut; they look bruised, like my fist when I punched Freddie that last day of school.

Freddie had no business sayin' what he did about Ma. But Teacher, she sure didn't see it that way.

Ma calls to me from the stove. "Torrie needs sleep, Jacob. Come eat while it's hot."

In a second I'm across the room in front of my porridge, sittin' beside Lizzy, opposite to Mr Cooper. I guess maybe I should be callin' him "Father Ed", like Victoria calls Ma "Mother Alice", but then he'd sound like a preacher.

Ma screeches a chair across the floor and

thump, her teacup is coverin' two red diamonds on the table oilcloth.

Usually Lizzy can't hush herself while we eat, but today she doesn't make a peep. We're all sittin' here quieter than barn cats at a mouse hole, waitin' for breakfast to come shootin' past.

My spoon hits the sugar bowl: ting! I dig in, heapin' the spoon with brown sugar that I dump in my hand and sprinkle over the oatmeal.

Lizzy shakes her head at me. "That's bad manners, Jacob."

"I know."

Ma sets her hot hand on mine, squeezin' my fingers hard. She never talks to me now she's Mrs Cooper – it's like she's not really my ma any more at all but a smithy, and I'm the piece of iron she's stuck in the fire to be shaped. She says there's no future in farmin', so workin' with Mr Cooper is best.

Mr Cooper clears his throat and turns his stare on me, so I keep my eyes on my bowl, pretendin' I don't see.

"When will Torrie be better?" Lizzy asks.

Ma leans over towards Lizzy, forgettin' all about me. "Maybe this afternoon. Then me and you'll have a tea party with her. Won't that be fun?"

"Can I be queen?" Lizzy asks. "Since she's turned thirteen, Torrie always gets to be Queen Victoria and I have to be princess."

Silently, I thank her for savin' me, and shove a spoonful of porridge into my mouth. Nobody can cook better than my ma.

"You'll be Queen Elizabeth," says Ma, smilin' at her. "But this mornin' we'll pull weeds, then come in out of the sun …"

Mr Cooper stops her and says, "If Victoria's not better tonight, Jacob can go for the doctor first thing tomorrow."

That makes my ears perk up. Mr Cooper does business with Mr Higgins so's he can use one of the horses whenever he needs it. I'd like drivin' his bay stallion over to Dawson for the doctor. But then I remember the last time I rode for the doctor – with Pa – back when I was ten. Dr Sam was no help at all. The flu still took both my older brothers.

Sharp on the mark of 7.45, Mr Cooper is stretchin' and standin' up. Even though I'm just as tall, I still feel half-growed beside him, instead of fifteen years old.

"Need anything brought back?" he asks Ma, same as every other day.

First she's shakin' her head, then thinks for a minute and says, "A tin of honey. For a cup of … tea for Torrie."

Mr Cooper nods, then leans down to pat Lizzy on the head. "Try to be quiet today, so Torrie can sleep."

Lizzy's curls bob up and down. "Yes, Papa," she agrees, reachin' up to hug him.

Ma stands, settin' the sack of lunch in my hands, then her fingers stretch to fasten the top button on my shirt.

"Ma …" I say, but think better of it and stop. Since Pa died, what I want has made about as much difference as a chicken flappin' its wings to escape Ma's axe in the autumn. She pulls the stiff white collar tight around my throat, chokin' the life right out of me.

Before we head out the door, I peer into the parlour – last night was the first I'd even seen behind those doors in the month since we've been livin' in this house. Victoria lies there, still as death.

Chapter Two

Outside, the sun is blisterin' the black dirt road. Back home, Uncle Charlie will be hitchin' the team to the mower after early chores. He's likely done the ten-acre field and moved on to the winter meadow by now.

Town's quiet this early, not like the farm. There's only the odd warblin' robin or thrush, and no caws of a crow or magpie. A sleek black dog lyin' on a doorstep we pass looks fat and lazy. Couldn't herd a sheep or cow out its own front gate.

Mr Cooper never says a word, just hurries past the houses lookin' straight ahead, like he's got nothin' to say to me. Uncle Charlie and me, we talked and talked and talked till I knew every story about him and Pa growin' up on the farm by heart.

I try to think about Pa as a boy like me – not crumpled up and caught in the cultivator, dead.

A cloud of dust flies off the slatted sidewalk in front of the Widow Pendleton's dry goods and millinery store. "Good morning, Ed, Jacob," she says, flickin' the broom back and forth.

Mr Cooper nods, stickin' his key in the green door of Cooper's General Hardware Store that's only a plough's width away.

"Good morning, Mrs Pendleton," I say, happy to stay in the street so we can chat about farmin'.

She stops and leans on a broom handle that's nearly half as wide as her. "It's a good one for making hay, isn't it? The boys were up and gone early," she says, talkin' about the three sons still livin' at home with her, even though they're all past twenty.

"Yes," I begin, but the look on Mr Cooper's face as he pushes the door open and turns to me tells me I best be right smart at followin'. "Have a good day," I say, forgettin' what I meant to ask.

The smell of the oiled wood floor closed in overnight smacks us in the face.

Mr Cooper gets right to business, pullin' the cover off the cash register and tossin' it under the dark pine counter that's twice as nice as the box we buried Pa in. "How many crates of stock are left to open?" Mr Cooper asks, pullin' out the daily ledger.

I stare down at my boots, wishin' I hadn't snuck off yesterday to see the horses instead of finishin' up my task in the back. Pa always told me if I couldn't give somethin' my best then I needed to think over what I was doin'. But Ma, well, she's of the opinion that some things just need gettin' on with, no matter what.

Mr Cooper lifts his head and stares at me, waitin' for an answer.

"There's three left, sir," I say, straightening my shoulders.

Anger shoots across Mr Cooper's face, pullin' the skin over his cheeks tight like leather. He says, "You only did one all afternoon?"

"Yes, sir," I say, not afraid of punishment. When I was small, it was either Teacher switchin' me for misbehavin' or Pa switchin' me for not payin' attention to what the teacher said.

We stare at each other like two roosters darin' the other one to make a move. The thought of Ma cryin' her eyes out again because I'm not tryin' hard enough makes me back down first.

Mr Cooper shakes his head and opens the ledger in front of him. "I need those hoe blades and flints, so find them first and bring them here. I'll price them."

"Yes, sir," I say again, almost wishin' he'd sent me home instead of back to the stock room.

The store is long and skinny with tin pails and

lanterns hangin' over the centre alleyway. "Twang, twang," clang the buckets in turn as my fingers bang each one on my way to the back. Behind the door sits a giant wooden crate that could hold a pony and two smaller, square crates.

Yesterday's pile of bridles and bits makes me homesick for Uncle Charlie and farmin' again. While I'm starin' at the heap, my teeth grind themselves together until I taste fresh blood from my bottom lip. I drop onto the three-legged stool to do my job.

When the church bells ring out for noon, I keep workin' until Mr Cooper opens the stock room door, looks around and says, "Time to eat."

It's hot inside the store, even hotter by the pot-bellied stove where steam pours from the silver tea kettle. A pot of last night's stew bubbles beside it, the smell makin' my stomach growl like a wild dog that hasn't eaten in days.

Before Mr Cooper can hand me the tin plates from the counter to fill, old Percy pushes through the door, keepin' hold on it to stop himself from fallin'. He croaks, "Wouldn't you know it, soon as I go to carve the trim for Mrs Petty's new chest of drawers, that darn blade on my old knife breaks."

Chapter Two

I'm wonderin' how he can still hold a knife the way his hand shakes.

"I'll fix you right up, Percy," Mr Cooper says cheerfully, then turns to me. "Jacob, make enough tea for Percy to have a cup, too."

I'd rather help old Percy, but I'm not allowed since I wrote in the wrong ledger row when Mrs Whalen was payin' her bill. She got right upset and screeched for Mr Cooper – he'd have found the mistake at closin' time anyway, so she didn't need to make such a fuss.

That was the nice part about bein' thrown out of school. Nobody to fuss at me, specially Annie Whyte – she made trouble every time I looked at her paper for the answers.

While Mr Cooper listens to old Percy talk about every piece of furniture he's ever made, I eat my stew and sip the tea that's already had time to steep. I can't help but wonder if Victoria's still lyin' in the parlour, lookin' so pale. She's the one should be workin' in the store, like her ma used to, instead o' me. Maybe then she wouldn't seem so sad all the time.

By the time Mr Cooper calls that we're ready to quit for the night, I've got the big crate emptied out and all the hardware laid in straight rows on the floor. But he doesn't even come back to check. The hardest part was matchin' the things up to the words on the bill, checkin' the store was sent the right amounts. Even when I know what the letters should say, it's not easy makin' it all work out in words. Numbers is easier. Any darn fool can count.

Mr Cooper opens the drawer on the cash register and pulls out some coins when I get to the front. "Get a tin of honey from the store," he says, droppin' them in my hand.

I'd forgotten Ma wanted honey for tea – she brought along all her dried herbs for nursin' when we came to town, and planted seeds in that new garden, same as when she came over from England. Honey takes the bitter out of those teas, so it will go down easy for Victoria.

"All right," I answer, glad for somethin' different to do.

My favourite thing in Wilson's Grocery is the smell of pickles that tickles my nose soon as I open the door. The wooden pickle barrels sit right up front by Mrs Wilson's pudgy left hand, ready for every kid with a penny to pick the plumpest, juiciest one.

"What'll you have today, Jacob?" she asks, her smilin' face round and red as an apple.

"Honey," I tell her, hopin' the coins jinglin' in my pocket cover the cost with a few pennies to spare.

"Over by the bags of flour," she says, pointin' me in the right direction.

I tramp over the store's green linoleum floor, past the cornmeal, bakin' powder, salt and stacks of flour. There's two sizes of honey on a white painted shelf – a pail and a tin, so I check my coins and take the smaller one.

Before the tin touches the counter, the cash register sings, "Ting, ting, ting." Mrs Wilson don't even ask, but takes the lid off the pickle barrel and presides over my choosin'.

I point at two floatin' in the barrel like tadpoles in a spring pond. The smallest pickles are always the best tastin'.

She fishes them out with her two-pronged, long-handled wooden fork and rolls them loose in brown paper. My mouth waters while I wait for her to dig up my change and hand it to me.

Plop. Crunch. The first one disappears before

I'm even outside, and the second follows right after. Two doors down, Mr Cooper is lockin' his business up.

The widow's youngest boy calls, "Whoa," and pulls his grey horse and wagon up to the hitchin' rail in front of her place.

I wave, wishin' I could stop to chat, but stretch my steps to catch up to Mr Cooper. "Here's your change, sir," I say, holdin' out the coins.

He takes a quick look and shakes his head. "You did a good job sorting the stock. Keep them."

I shove them in my pocket, addin' up in my head how much money I have already.

The church bells chime out six o'clock, coverin' my thanks, while we walk wordlessly home for supper. Around us, dust hangs in the heat, makin' it hard to breathe.

Ma's waitin' on the doorstep, her face white as milk. "Torrie is worse," she calls, before we even open the gate into the yard.

Mr Cooper turns ash-grey and whirls around without a word, headin' back down the street towards Mr Higgins' place. I expect he's goin' for the doctor himself.

CHAPTER 3
Victoria

A voice – Jacob's – whispers words that skip, like a rock on water, through my mind. "… all right … your papa … soon … doctor."

Lightning bolts, red-hot streaks of pain, fork through my legs, twisting and twitching down their length.

Terrified, I scream.

My fingernails dig into a hand, claw past pencil-thin fingers to leathery palms … and stop. There's something wrong. These aren't my mama's hands.

"Mama? Where are you, Mama? I need you."

"Shush," someone whispers. "Just shush and close your eyes."

I do.

Sleep carries me away and I'm a little girl

again, first day of school, braids hanging down my back, Papa whispering, "You can do it, Victoria, you can do it."

"No, I can't," I shout.

"You can," someone whispers.

School again – a teacher pulling my hair into a topknot to hold the crown. Queen Victoria's crown. Margaret, my best friend from our first day of school, her skirt held high, curtseys for me, the queen.

A boy from the graduating class, his scrubbed face serious, dips to one knee on the golden hardwood floor. My voice, solemn and strong: "I knight thee Sir William Thomson, in recognition of your work in laying the first transatlantic cable …"

The curtain closes, hands clap and the choir sings. Margaret's voice sounds above it, leading the others: "Hail, Britannia, Britannia rules the waves …" After, she laughs and tells me to enjoy my day of being queen, for it won't likely happen again.

My thigh twitches against the cotton sheet, against my command. How can I be queen when my own body ignores me and spasms in streaks of pain?

My eyes open and gaze into Mother Alice's.

"Torrie," she whispers, voice half iron, half goose-down feathers, "sip this tea," and presses an Allerton's china cup to my mouth, so Mama's pink English roses touch my lips.

The liquid flows into my mouth. My tongue darts past cracked lips, curls and spits, so tea splatters on Mother Alice's cheek.

That wasn't what I meant to do.

Margaret skips through my mind – a tea party for my ninth birthday, a shattered plate, cake crumbs on the floor.

My body crumbles, broken.

"Let me try, Ma," says Jacob, face flickering in my eyes, like a candle flame about to die.

The china cup touches my lips again and rests against the cracks. This time I'm ready for the taste when the tea trickles over them, welcome rivulets on parched flesh.

"Can you taste the ginger and honey?" Jacob whispers as he tips the cup another time. "It's sweet to hide the taste of wolfsbane."

An image of Mother Alice plucking plants from the meadow floor, digging roots and dropping them one by one into a witch's cauldron, stirring and chanting as the fire heats, dances before me. Whose wicked stepmother is she – Cinderella's, Sleeping Beauty's, Rapunzel's, mine?

The garden – Mother Alice's garden. A thistle poked my finger there. Had she cast a spell on it? Dropped poison on its tip? Bewitched me?

My eyelids droop and my face, where I touch it, burns.

I whirl into a world of dwarfs and witches, where the sceptre with my power lies useless on the floor. They dance, with Mother Alice, round and round and round the fire, spinning, spinning, spinning …

Jacob's voice shatters the glass cage around me – shards fly off in all directions, dissolving the flames. "Victoria, you need to drink some more," he says.

I do.

When I open my eyes again, the witch is gone and Mother Alice sits in the rosewood chair, her hands clasped, as if in prayer.

What does she know of nursing? She can't read or write or use fine manners or do fancy needlework or put her own hair up in a topknot. How can she know what will make me well?

Pain is everywhere.

The dull throb that hammered in my head has moved, tiptoed down my body, lodged in the small of my back. Why, I wonder? The last thing I lifted was light – the basket of wet sheets that dried on the line the day I watched Jacob run through the meadow.

I see him now, stretched on the floor, resting, head on a pillow, one finger twined in the carpet's red fringe, ready to do his mother's bidding.

Are they waiting for me to die?

"Where's Papa?" I ask, my voice raspy, as if a file has roughened my throat. Each word sucks the air out of me, leaving me gasping for more.

Heavy eyelids lift and Mother Alice's eyes blink to life. "How do you feel?" she asks.

I don't answer, but ask again, "Where's Papa?"

"Gone for the doctor," says Jacob, kneeling beside the sofa, close enough for me to see the fear in his eyes, even in the feeble glow of the electric lights shining through the doors.

Mother Alice disappears to the kitchen.

A dagger twists and stabs me again.

"My back … hurts," I gasp.

Papa will bring the doctor through the moonlit night, but I think how long it took for him to come to Mama – too long. The midwife had covered her face by then.

The question "Will I die?" burns in my head, and I hear Mama's strong soprano in the church: "A-ma-zing grace, how sweet the sound …" But it isn't Sunday, and I'm not ready to leave, not ready yet to be with Mama or the little brother I never knew.

Jacob says, "Try not to think about the pain. Don't let it rule you."

I nod. Victoria rules, she isn't ruled.

"Flowers," he says, the word rolling from his tongue, like a marble across the floor. "Think of flowers, fields of flowers."

I do.

I've spilled my paint tray in the grass, each drop a blob of colour that springs to life and blooms – I drink up the smells, brush my fingers over soft velvet petals, curl my toes around stems and leaves and vines. And there I am, racing away from pain, and the angel of death.

Chapter Three

Mother Alice turns me on my side, rubs my back and eases the twitching of my legs, until my eyes close.

"Do you need a bedpan?" she whispers, while Jacob is in his garret room.

"No!" I cry, then try to rise but can't.

The cold pewter pan beneath me brings tears to my eyes, tears of embarrassment. I wonder why she has such a thing, but keep the question to myself, thankful she does.

The hours pass and the electric lights go out. I drink. Sleep.

Try to drink again, but the tea trickles in, then back out through my nose – burns and splatters down my face. Breathe. Gasp for air, but it's too heavy. I can't suck it in.

There's a strange noise.

Moaning.

Me.

Jacob's voice says, "Try not to cry out. I've a kettle of boilin' water for steam, to help your throat."

Wet cloudy air fills the space around me, licks at my lips and my tongue and my throat and finally wriggles through.

Another sip of tea. My eyes are too heavy to stay awake.

I hurt too much.

The room whirls around two candles that glow on the sofa table. Water bubbles far away, boiling on the stove, ready to refill the pot that's grown cold beside me.

It's too hard to talk, too hard even to cry.

My foot cramps, arches full-length, toes curled, pointing at the floor, and a thousand needles race down the stretched skin, two-by-two, like animals on Noah's ark, with everything left behind dying.

It must be late. Where's Papa?

The spasms go on forever, twisting my foot, my toes, my mind. When one stops, another begins – the torture goes on and on, and I'm lost in it.

Mother Alice blows the night's candles out, while the sun, ashamed of what the day may bring, hides behind thick clouds. Elizabeth calls, half asleep, from the bedroom, "Is Torrie better yet?" Jacob runs to soothe her.

Thunder rolls and the parlour grows darker. Morning rain pounds on the window pane, rat-a-tat-tat, rat-a-tat-tat, then slows, tap-tap, tap-tap.

"Breathe in, breathe out," I command. Think only of air not pain. "Breathe in, breathe out." And my body does.

The door bangs against the kitchen wall and someone arrives. Elizabeth shouts, "Papa!"

Heavy footsteps and a deep voice tell me he has the doctor with him.

But when I see him, it's not Dr Sam, who came for Mama, but someone young, his red face hiding behind a dark moustache.

Papa says, "Dr Oliver's here, Torrie. He'll make you well."

"I'm here to help you," says the doctor, bending so the stethoscope hangs over me, swinging out of reach. "Your papa's told me a little, but I'd like you to tell me more." His hand, cold and damp as a cloth, touches my forehead.

"It hurts … so bad," I gasp.

"Yes, of course," he mutters, fingers prodding my throat. "Where does it hurt?"

"All over," I say, trying not to cry.

"Victoria, you're a big girl. Surely you can be clearer than that," the doctor says, stethoscope touching my skin.

I wince from his words, add them to my pain.

Mother Alice lifts the blanket as another spasm twists my foot and a whimper escapes my lips.

The doctor watches. "What treatment have you given?" he asks Mother Alice.

"It seemed a little like the croup at first, even without the cough, so I gave her honey tea with ginger and wolfsbane," Mother Alice says, gently covering my legs.

"Wolfsbane!" cries the doctor. "What kind of witchery is this? Wolfsbane is a dire poison – we're lucky she's still alive."

"'Tis a good medicine, used well," says Mother Alice, not withering under the doctor's stare. "In England, in the convent, it was a favourite of Sister Mary's."

My head whirls and I wonder, did I dream her chanting over a witch's cauldron, or hear her in the moonlight?

Papa's voice, grim, says coldly, "You'll use only what the doctor orders now, Alice."

She nods. "Whatever you and Victoria wish."

The doctor goes on, prodding my body, each

touch making me cry with pain. He reaches my feet and says, "Can you wiggle your toes?"

What a foolish question, I think, until I try.

While my throat closes with fear, my toes refuse to move. I shut my eyes and I hear Mama's voice chanting: "This little piggy went to market, and this little piggy stayed home. This little piggy had roast beef, and this little piggy had none. And this little piggy went 'wee-wee-wee', all the way home." As her warm fingers caress each toe in my memory, I try again to move them.

But I can't.

The doctor asks, "Can you lift your leg?"

I don't want to know, but, tears streaming down my face, I try.

Nothing happens.

"The other one?" he says.

I try again, imagine I'm ten, my feet thumping the ground over a jumping rope. "Barber, barber, shave a pig, how many hairs will make a wig …" chants Margaret.

Papa says slowly, his voice as distant as Margaret's, "Not that one either?"

There's no answer.

"What's wrong?" whispers Elizabeth. "What happened to Torrie's legs?"

I hear Papa lift her into his arms, murmur that she's his special girl.

The doctor plods around the sofa, poking me here and there – my left arm moves, and my right arm moves, and both my hands move, and each of my fingers moves, one by one.

"Infantile paralysis," Dr Oliver announces, as calmly as if I've just had too much sun after all. "It appears to be affecting her legs, mostly. There is little I can do but splint the affected muscles tight and immobilise them to keep them from moving."

Papa gasps, as if a giant bellows is squeezing the air out of him. "Are you sure?" he asks.

"I am," says the doctor. The latch on his medical bag clicks open and his cold hands begin the torture of twisting my foot against splints, wrapping them tight, until I scream with agony.

Mother Alice says, "Surely giving her more pain won't help, will … ?"

"We do what the doctor orders," says Papa, chopping off her words.

CHAPTER 4
JACOB

My head's been spinnin' since the doctor poked Victoria in the foot and said those awful words – "infantile paralysis". What if it was me lyin' there, instead of her?

"Whoa," I call, pullin' on the reins. Mr Higgins' old black mare stops quick, tired after the three-hour drive to Dawson. Beside me, the doctor jumps awake, so the cap over his eyes flies off.

"Thank you, Jacob," says Dr Oliver, climbin' out of the buggy and pullin' his doctor bag after himself. "Now, if there are no babies needing assistance coming into the world, no accidents or injuries and nobody sick, maybe I can catch a few hours of sleep lying down for a change."

I nod. "Thanks for comin'," I say, as polite as

I can. After he called Ma's tea witchery, I'm not of a mind to be friendly.

The train whistle blows and buries whatever Dr Oliver says before he heads into his office. Mr Higgins' mare isn't used to the sound, so she starts prancin', stirrin' up the dust on the wide main street. As the steam engine gets closer, the clang-clang-clang of its wheels and the squealin' eek of the brakes make her even more skittish.

It's well past noon, so there's no use hurryin' back to town, since the store will be closed up by the time I get back. I've only been to Dawson twice before, so the thought of explorin' it keeps me from feelin' too tired.

"Giddup," I call, shakin' the reins. The mare plods ahead, tired out, even though it's clouded up and cooler today. First stop is the Nicholson Drug Store, to get more of the pain medicine the doctor gave Victoria.

A wagon rolls out of the Mathews Dray Lines business, a load of stock stacked up so high the team of four big Clydesdale horses has to strain to keep it movin'. The drayman waves at me and I think of those crates still left to empty back at the store.

Chapter Four

We pass the saddle and harness shop, the livery stables, Park Rooming House, Bielen Hotel, the Brockman dentist office and Tanner Hall. There's more than a thousand people lives in Dawson, so it's busy enough for two smithy shops, two general stores and even a farm implement place.

At the chemist shop, a little man peers over the wire rim of his glasses at me and asks, "What can I get you, son?"

I hand him the piece of paper the doctor gave me. "This is for Victoria Cooper. The doctor says she's got infantile paralysis."

"Poor little Victoria." A look of concern crosses his face, then turns curious. "Didn't Mrs Cooper die last autumn?" he asks.

"Yes," I say.

He stares at me through the glasses, eyes nearly crossin', until he finally says, "You must be the Moore boy – your ma just married Ed Cooper, didn't she?"

"Yes," I say again, not addin' anythin' else. Pa always said a tight lip makes a wise man out of a fool.

The pharmacist gives up starin' at me and says, "It'll be ten minutes or so until I can get this mixed up." He turns, fingers runnin' over labels on the jars and jars of powders on ruler-straight shelves behind his counter. Even with his back turned, he keeps talkin'.

"Folks in Dawson are sure enough happy that young Dr Oliver's here, helping Dr Sam. The lad's fresh from Guy's Hospital Medical School in London, he is, and doing quite a job. Mrs Black credits him with saving her young lad's leg that got hurt when his horse reared. And old Peter Davies, well, he swears he's been cured of the gout."

So far, I figure, besides namin' what Victoria's got, he hasn't been of much help to us. As soon as the pharmacist stops talkin' I look around.

Stickin' my left hand in my pocket, I feel each of the half-dozen coins of my own I've brought along. Money isn't somethin' Ma and I saw much of on the farm. Before Pa died, things were hard, but after, they were worse. Finally, Ma turned it all over to Uncle Charlie to farm with his land when there was no money to pay him for his work.

My feet clip-clop over the floorboards as I walk around the little shop, wonderin' what might be good to buy. There's a big cupboard full o' bottles and bottles of Dr Ordinaire's elixir that promises to cure whatever ails you. I think about buyin' it for a minute to try for Victoria, but figure since the doctor didn't order it, her pa wouldn't have none of it anyway.

My steps take me to the far end of the wooden counter and I see somethin' I have to buy – red-and-white striped peppermint sticks. I'll take some back for Ma and Lizzy, too.

A little bell chimes as the door opens and a lady in a pink dress is towed in by a boy near the size of Lizzy. It only takes him a second to wriggle out of her grip and dart across the floor towards me.

"No, Anthony," calls the lady.

The man behind the counter turns in time to see the boy grab a long candy stick from the box and shove it in his mouth.

I'm expectin' the drug store man to yell, but instead he laughs. "Well, well. How's my favourite grandson today," he says, droppin' the jars he's mixin' from.

"You shouldn't encourage him, Dad," says the lady, shakin' her head so the little ringlets hangin' down the side of her face brush over her white lacy collar.

"Come to Grandad," he says, wobblin' out from behind the counter and kneelin' on the floor.

Anthony shrieks, runs across the room and throws his arms around the man, smearin' the wrinkled old face with red candy streaks.

I shuffle out of the way, thinkin' about what it would have been like to have grandparents. Ma grew up in an orphanage in England and agreed to marry Pa before she even met him. Pa's family had been here for most of a hundred years. Him and Uncle Charlie shared up the land when their pa died, put up another house, a ways from the first, and their sisters married, moved away. I always thought I'd take over someday. But Ma's made other plans.

Little Anthony opens a door to the back and scoots through, shoutin' for his grandma. That's when I notice the little sign that says *Mrs Perkins Dressmaking* hangin' over it. Anyway, they all disappear through the door and I'm alone in the store, wonderin' what to do next.

I glance around the room again and spy some books through the glass front of the counter.

There's four lyin' there, and I think of Victoria and how much she loves readin'.

The picture on the biggest book must be a puppet show – Ma's talked about seein' one at the orphanage. *Chatterbox* is written across the top, over the year 1911. One of the puppets is beatin' the other with a stick, while a policeman is bent over. The book is thick as two slices o' Ma's bread, so would likely take even Victoria a long time to read.

I know the words on the next one, since it's *The Farmer's Almanac*. Teacher had a new one every year, so she could tell folks when to plant the crops and gardens. The new teacher that came last year must, too, since Uncle Charlie's visited her every week since winter.

The book after that is small and white and square – *The Tale of Timmy Tiptoes*. It takes a bit to figure out the words, but the cover shows me the story's about a squirrel gatherin' nuts.

But it's the last book that appears to be the most interestin'. The book is opened up, showin' a fella who looks like he's made out of a tin pail, and another fella with dancin' feet who looks like a scarecrow. The title's in big letters and not too bad to spell out: *The Wonderful Wizard of Oz*.

The longer I stare at the book, the curiouser and curiouser I get about the story inside. It must be about Oz, whatever kind of place that is, I figure, lookin' at the book title. Then I work out the words, "The funniest child's book …" and think it would be good to make Victoria smile, forget about the pain.

"Ready, young fella?" says the old man.

I nearly jump out of my boots at the sound! I nod and mutter, "How much is the medicine?"

After I've counted out what it costs from the money Mr Cooper gave me, I ask for ten peppermint sticks and hand him some of my pennies. I've still a little handful left.

"Is that everything?" he asks, droppin' the coins into the cash drawer.

I suck in a deep breath and say, "How much for the *Oz* book? I think Victoria would like it." There's somethin' about that story makes me feel maybe I can learn to read it to Victoria – if I try hard, maybe she'll only have to help me a little.

"Well …" he says, like he's thinkin' hard, "it's already been read once, so I guess I could give it to you for a good price. How much do you have?"

I stick out my hand with the leftover coins.

He bends down, slides the wooden door on his side of the counter open and pulls out the book. "That looks about enough to cover the cost."

The book feels heavy when he sets it in my hand, like it's more important than the tiny bottle of medicine I pick up with my other one.

The miles pass slowly on my way back to town and I'm half asleep, hunched over on the seat. Clip-clop, clip-clop, clip-clop. Lucky thing the old mare just keeps ploddin' on toward home.

I leave the horse and buggy at Mr Higgins' and walk across town to our place. It's quiet except for a crack of thunder. At the house I'm half afraid to open the door — scared things are worse instead of better inside.

Ma's at the stove, fillin' the kettle with water. Mr Cooper's sittin' next to Victoria, his chin restin' on his chest. Lizzy isn't anywhere.

"I brought the medicine," I say, handin' it to

Ma, along with Mr Cooper's money.

She shakes her head and I can tell she don't put no stock in it helpin' any. So far, she's done as good at nursin' as any doctors I've seen, even if that Dr Oliver don't think so.

"Thank you, Jacob," she says, her voice low.

I glance around the room again.

"I brought some peppermint sticks for you and Lizzy. Where is she?"

Ma rubs a hand across her brow. "Playing with her dollies on her bed, so Victoria can sleep. But she'll be glad to have you back for company."

Anxious to share the treat, I head to the bedroom without callin', so I don't wake Mr Cooper. At the door I stop. There's Lizzy, lyin' in bed, her face near as red as the dress on her rag doll.

"Ma," I call out, not careful any longer. "Lizzy looks sick."

Ma hurries past me and lays her hand on Lizzy's forehead. Mr Cooper shoves into the room, pushin' me to the side.

"Not my Lizzy, too," he says, his voice crackin'.

"Wet some cloths, Jacob," says Ma. "Cold ones. She's fevered." She doesn't answer Mr Cooper.

Chapter Four

I put the book and candy away in the kitchen, wishin' the day could end now and start over with tomorrow the same as things were two days ago.

"Jacob," calls Victoria from the parlour, "is something wrong with Elizabeth?"

"It's a fever – like yours," I answer, givin' her the plain truth. That's what I'd want if I was her.

"Oh …" she says. "I wish I could do something." She turns her head away and I know she's cryin'.

"I can do whatever needs doin'," I say. "Just try to close your eyes. Your pa's goin' for the doctor again at daybreak."

There's no sleep happens in the house as night comes. Rain starts poundin' on the window and the thunder keeps boomin' and lightnin' streaks through the sky. It feels like we're all stuck in a nightmare and can't wake up.

We take turns, Ma and me, lyin' cloths on Lizzy's head for the fever and tryin' to get her to drink somethin', listenin' to her scream in pain while her breathin' gets worse and worse. Her pa moves back and forth, from her bed to Victoria out in the parlour.

After a while, I heat up some soup for a supper in the candlelight, since the electricity don't come on like it should. The soup's full of bits of potatoes and carrots swimmin' in chicken broth, but I can hardly taste it at all from worryin' about the infantile paralysis.

"Can you eat some soup, Victoria?" I ask when I notice her eyes open up again.

"I'll try," she says. "I have to get better to help with Elizabeth."

While I'm gettin' a fresh bowl of soup, I try not to think about little Lizzy, lyin' sick in the other room. I'm not a nurse like Ma, but I could see she's even worse than Victoria last night.

I prop some pillows behind Victoria, but just liftin' her that little bit makes her cry out with pain. "I'm sorry," I say.

"It's all right — there doesn't seem to be any way to move that doesn't hurt," she says, blinkin' tears out of her eyes. She tries to use the spoon herself, but her hand comes up off the sofa a little ways and drops down quick. At least it isn't paralysed, like her legs.

I don't say nothin', just lift the spoon to offer it. Her mouth opens, like a baby bird's, waitin' for the soup. The first spoonful is too full and some drools out the edge of her mouth, so I wipe it away with a cloth.

"Sorry," I say. "I'll make the next one half full."

She nods and we try again.

As I wait for her to swallow, I start talkin', tellin' her about the baby animals I've helped nurse, while she stays quiet, just workin' at eatin'.

"The year before Pa died he came in one day with his hand coverin' his hat. Turned out he had five little rabbits, orphaned when their ma hopped in front of the plough to protect her burrow. Course he couldn't leave them to starve, so he brought them in."

"What happened?" says Victoria, turning her head from the spoon. She hasn't eaten as much as one of those baby rabbits.

"Ma and I nursed all five of 'em till they got big enough in the autumn to turn back loose. They stayed awake every night, hoppin' round our two-room house, followin' one another and playin' games. Pa and I used to sit quiet, just watchin' 'em have fun …" I stop there. Thinkin' of Pa hasn't made me feel this much like cryin' for a long time now.

Victoria doesn't say nothin', but I guess she's thinkin' about her ma.

Then I remember the book and leap to my feet, makin' sure not to spill the bit of soup left in the bowl. In a few steps I'm back at the sofa with it, showin' Victoria the cover.

"I thought, well, I could maybe try readin' it to you, you know, while you're sick."

She tries to smile. "*The Wonderful Wizard of Oz.* It looks exciting," she says. "Thank you, Jacob."

As soon as I give her a bit of the doctor's medicine, she's ready to sleep again, so I see if Ma needs me to help her with Lizzy. But she and Mr Cooper are both sittin' there, side by side, watchin' her and holdin' her weak little hands.

I can see Mr Cooper's not goin' to leave his baby, so I figure he'll help Ma for the night and I should just crawl up the ladder to the garret and look at the pictures in the Oz book. Even though I'm tired, I don't get much sleep, because my eyes pop open every time I roll or hear a noise, like they always do in this house.

A shriek from below wakes me up somewhere

around sunrise. Pullin' on my trousers, I drop down onto the kitchen floor and hurry into the bedroom. Ma's there, tears rollin' down her cheeks, pullin' the sheet over Lizzy's little face, while Mr Cooper sits beside her, shakin' with giant sobs.

CHAPTER 5
Victoria

Sobs, Papa's sobs, yank me from my dreams, but it's Jacob's face, wet behind a waterfall of tears, that tells me the worst has happened: our darling Elizabeth has gone to Mama – gone to rest in her arms, not ours.

A spasm grabs me, jerks my leg, rips from toe to heart and leaves me crying for myself and Papa and Jacob and Mother Alice. What will I do now, without Elizabeth? What will they do?

As I squeeze my eyes shut, I see a tiny angel – cherubic face and snow-white wings – hover, touch Mama's photo on the wall above me and Grandmother Cooper's, too. The angel smiles.

"Victoria …" murmurs Jacob, dropping onto his knees beside the sofa, his brown eyes staring into mine.

"I know," I whisper back.

Chapter Five

Jacob struggles to his feet, crosses the kitchen, and disappears into the garret – his refuge.

"Take care of her, Mama. Take care of baby Elizabeth," I whisper, too weak to turn my face.

The sun rises and the room fills with light, but life doesn't go on. Nobody goes to open Papa's store. Nobody makes porridge and tea. Nobody speaks their grief. I wish Margaret were here to talk with me, not gone to her aunt's to help with the twins.

My cheeks burn with fever and my legs, held tight in the doctor's wraps, throb with each heartbeat. I won't give in to the pain and yowl with agony, so I gnaw on my sheet like a dog on a bone, until at last my strength is gone. My eyes close and I fall into a restless sleep.

I awake to the acrid smell of something boiling on the stove. Mother Alice dips her arm into the cauldron and pulls a thin, dripping cloth, hung on a wooden spoon, from the tin wash boiler. It's streaked with black – she drops it back.

She glances at me and asks, "Are you thirsty, Torrie?"

"What's that?" I croak, my mind foggy with sleep and pain.

"Black dye," she says, without a blink, "for mourning clothes."

Mother Alice doesn't say, "I'm sorry your sister's gone." She doesn't say, "I know how you must feel." She doesn't say, "I wish I could do something for your loss." Instead, she plunges the spoon into the depths of the dye, stirs, goes about the business of death like she's hilling potatoes in the garden, heaping black dirt over whatever grew below.

Jacob drops from the ladder, puts one arm around his mother's shoulders, takes the spoon from her with the other and prods the cloth. They stand together. Where is Papa to hold my hand? Wipe my tears? Take away my pain?

I cry a silent whimper and Jacob comes, spoons the doctor's medicine, mixed with sugar, into my mouth. The pain dulls, so I drift away in sleep.

Later, after the bedpan, Mother Alice lifts me, turns me, puts a ryegrass straw to my lips. A nectar that tastes of lemon and honey fills my mouth, chills my aching throat and quenches my thirst. I sleep again.

It's near nightfall before I hear papa's voice.

"Jacob," he calls. "Help bring in the coffin."

Chapter Five

Jacob appears, with Mother Alice following behind, carrying a small, dripping wet flannel in her hand.

The door opens.

Mr Turner, the new cabinetmaker, blocks the entrance with his bulk, holding back the last light of the day. Even so, it's the small brown box, circled by a band of angels playing harps, that fills the room.

Papa is silent, his face a stone.

Everyone turns to look at me, lying in the parlour. This is where the coffin goes. Where Elizabeth's body must rest before the burial. What of me?

Mother Alice is the first to speak. "Torrie, the bedroom …"

"I can't," I shout, as loudly as my sore throat allows. "I can't sleep there …" And my voice falls to a plea. "Not yet." I think of all the nights my baby sister snuggled close and tears wet my eyes, my lashes, my cheeks.

Jacob, quiet until now, says, "Can't we … just … move the sofa … to the kitchen."

We all stare at Papa, waiting. Waiting for him to decide what's to be done with me. "Move the table, Jacob," he says. "Make room in here for Torrie."

Mother Alice pulls back the wooden chairs and helps push the table to the side, while Papa and Mr Turner stay still. I watch, dreading the moment when they shift me and the sofa and place the coffin where I am now.

By the time I'm settled under the kitchen window, dusk has fallen. There is no moon, no stars, no sounds of night outside, not yet.

I am alone.

Hushed voices creep through the house, touching it with sadness. "Which dress … yellow … her hair …"

Propped up against the sofa back, my face sinking in soft pillows, I watch as Papa cradles Elizabeth in his arms, carries her to the coffin, her final resting place.

Mother Alice waits there.

I imagine the satin – white and smooth – that lines the wooden box and wish I could see it, touch it, cry tears over it, instead of lying here, with paralysed legs, pain shooting through me.

Papa's shoulders heave with silent sobs as he bends and lays Elizabeth down.

Chapter Five

Jacob stands aside, left out, as Papa and Mother Alice clasp hands across the coffin.

"She is so beautiful," whispers Mother Alice, staring down.

Papa nods.

But I lie here, an ocean of tears away from them all, by myself. The electric lights flicker, die early, just like Elizabeth.

When morning comes, I hear the twittering of birds outside the kitchen window, feel sunshine on my face and think that this is a nicer day.

The stove lid clangs as Mother Alice lifts it, shoves in some wood, blows on the embers and brings the fire crackling back to life. How easy it all seems from where I watch.

"Good morning, Torrie," she says. "Better this morning?"

I don't answer, but I check for myself. Toes? They don't wiggle. Legs? They don't lift at all. I'm still too weak to roll from back to side, and pain fogs my brain.

"No," I say, my voice sharp as a tack – as mean as Sam from next door's taunts when I miss my sums. "I want to be turned," I mutter, waiting.

Mother Alice comes. Her hands, businesslike

and brisk, roll me like bread dough.

I want to say thank you, but I can't, not now.

Later, all garbed in black, they talk over tea and biscuits – Papa, Mother Alice and Jacob. Planning.

Mother Alice gestures at me and says, "She's much too ill and weak to go to the funeral."

I clamp my eyes closed, feign sleep.

Before they're done, the Reverend Scott knocks and steps inside. He, too, is dressed in black, the colour of death. "I'm sorry for your loss," he says, nodding at Mother Alice.

"Thank you for coming, Reverend," says Papa. "What else needs taking care of?"

Yesterday, Papa would have gone to church, knelt in our pew and offered a prayer before they spoke. Today, the Reverend asks questions and Papa answers. The ceremony is planned. Hymns are chosen, coffin-carriers named.

"Jacob," says Papa. "Go and see Mr Higgins to rent his hearse for the procession, for our Elizabeth's last ride."

Jacob nods and stands. He's out through the door without a word. I watch, angry that I'm the one lying here while he runs away, escapes.

Chapter Five

Later, I close my eyes when he brings the book to share. I can't think of anything but pain.

The day passes and another begins. Evil spasms grow stronger in my legs, twisting my feet against their prison. Each spoonful of medicine spreads clouds of wool through my head and takes less of the agony away.

After lunch, Mr Beston comes through the kitchen door, camera in hand, to take Elizabeth's last picture. "I'm sorry for your loss," he says to Mother Alice, then nods at me.

I try not to stare at his face with its canyons of pock-marks scarring suntanned skin. Are they what brings him to his Kodak, seeking beauty behind the lens to make up for what he's lost in the mirror?

What scars will infantile paralysis leave me?

Mother Alice pushes back the doors, where the coffin sits balanced between two blood-red chairs. "Here's Elizabeth," she says as she lights the lamps around the room.

"So peaceful," Mr Beston says, stepping through the arch.

The Kodak opens. A red accordion falls from the black metal box and the silver eye in front takes aim. One click far away takes in the coffin and one click closer up the yellow lilies at its side.

Mr Beston says, "We will need to set down the coffin."

Mother Alice nods and calls, "Jacob, can you help us."

Jacob descends the ladder, glances at me, then helps Mr Beston lean one end upright against the chair, sets the other gently on the floor, and drops to his knees to hold it there.

For the first time, I see Elizabeth's sleeping face across the room. Tears cloud my eyes and I cry.

Mr Beston points the Kodak – click-click, click-click.

The minutes crawl past while memories fly on angel wings: her first steps, from my arms to Papa's; her chubby little hands clutching crumpled dandelions for Mama in the store; her wicker carriage rattling over the slatted sidewalk, pushing china doll Annie; her monotone voice filling our pew at church: "There's a friend for little children, above the bright blue sky … "

As my hands cover my face, I hear Jacob move the coffin, close the room, say goodbye to Mr Beston at the door.

My sobbing tires me and I drift off to sleep again, dreaming of Margaret and school – days gone by and days yet to come.

The last day of school flickers in and out like a candle and I watch the three-legged race where we ran, stumbling together, across the playground. I reach for the first-prize ribbon, but it disappears and I find myself at Margaret's house, watching her pack her bags for the summer at her aunt's.

I roll and wonder if I'll ever feel our legs tied together, stuck in a sack, running a race again.

The day disappears without anything changing at all. Papa comes and goes, but never stops to talk or hold my hand. Jacob and Mother Alice spoon food into my mouth, hold ryegrass straws to my lips, so I can suck water and tea, shift my body when it aches and measure out medicine that barely numbs the pain.

Night falls. Twinkling stars fill the sky. A chorus of creatures harmonises beyond the window glass, without the benefit of Mama's piano, which sits silent inside, behind the doors.

Mr Higgins' stallion pulls the hearse up to our house, sun glinting off silver trim, when the church bells ring. The animal neighs, paws a foot.

Papa calls, his voice flat, like a penny coin that's lost its face. "Jacob, come help."

Together, they carry the coffin – my baby sister's coffin – through the house, down the steps and away. I watch her ride down the street, past the houses, until the carriage disappears and the dust settles. Will I ever walk to her grave? Run my fingers over her headstone? See where she rests, next to Mama?

Mother Alice brings medicine one more time – I shake my head. No. I'd rather feel pain than hazy clouds of nothing at all.

She stands beside Papa, black skirt over the tops of her leather boots, looking tired and worn. Papa walks stiffly, helping her into Mr Higgins' small carriage to follow the hearse's path to church. Jacob trails, climbs in, settles by his mother.

I watch through the glass and wait.

Chapter Five

At last, the final procession rolls up the street. No birds tweet, no children shout, no dogs bark. It's long – the hearse, Mr Higgins' carriage, nine buggies, five wagons, everyone dressed in black. A cloud, dark and heavy, drifts over the sun, casting a shadow over it all.

In the silence, I open my mouth to sing my sister home to Mama, softly at first, then stronger, even as my voice cracks.

"The Lord has promis'd good to me,
His word my hope secures;
He will my shield and portion be,
As long as life endures."

The house aches with silence when they return. Mother Alice changes into a housedress, then disappears to run her fingers through the garden soil. At the table Jacob sits, puzzling out words in the book before him.

Papa, my papa, sips his tea and stares at the parlour doors, shut on an empty room.

CHAPTER 6
JACOB

Mr Cooper's sittin' alone at the table after supper and I wonder why he don't pull his chair over beside Victoria, at the sofa. Little Lizzy's gone, but Victoria's fightin' the infantile paralysis and soundin' stronger every day, even though she's hurtin' bad. I figure it's not my place to ask, so I move my chair over instead.

Her eyes are open, so I ask, "Are you feelin' well enough to hear me readin' *The Wonderful Wizard of Oz*?" I hold up the book to show her the cover again, in case she forgot about it with the fever.

She nods.

Before I begin, I whisper, quiet as a cricket afraid to sing, "The church hymns today were real nice, like angels takin' Lizzy to your ma."

"I'm glad," she whispers back, keepin' her eyes on the book.

The first lines of the story make me think of home, back before Pa died, with Dorothy's Uncle Henry and Aunt Em all livin' in two little rooms. "What's c-y-c-l-o-n-e say?" I ask, since I had to skip it readin' to myself when I was practisin'.

Victoria smiles a little. "That's a cyclone. You know, a big wind that comes down out of the sky in a funnel and sucks up everything in its path."

So I read her how the book describes the house and cyclone. *"There was no garret at all, and no cellar – except a small hole dug in the ground, called a cyclone cellar, where the family could go in case one of those great whirlwinds arose, mighty enough to crush any building in its path."*

"Can you imagine a wind like that?" she asks.

I shake my head. "I felt big winds, but none that would rip away a house or a barn."

So on I read, imaginin' everything grey and flat in Kansas, where Dorothy lives. Words don't seem to be so hard when they're stuck between other ones, instead of lyin' alone on a page. These words make pictures in my head, so when I blink I can see Toto the dog, with his long, black, silky hair and small black eyes and funny wee nose.

Victoria lies still, eyes mostly closed, helpin' me when I have to spell out hard words or strange words. Some of these I never heard before.

Ma comes and listens to me read, slow like an ox ploddin' step by step through mud, instead of a fast horse runnin' over grass. I'm wishin' Victoria was well enough to do the readin', not waitin' for me. I want to get the story quick.

Finally, Ma says, "Victoria must be tired. She'd best sleep now."

"But, Ma," I say, not ready to stop.

She runs her fingers through my hair, like she used to when I was small.

"Just one more line," I plead.

She nods.

I read, "*'Quick, Dorothy!' she screamed. 'Run for the cellar!'*" and turn to Ma. "But, Ma, it's a cyclone comin'. I know it's a cyclone."

"It must be," says Victoria, turning her head to us. "What else could that sharp whistling in the air and bending grass be?"

"Sure sounds like a cyclone," says Ma, "and tomorrow we'll find out for sure."

Chapter Six

I close the book, knowin' that Ma never changes her mind.

Outside the window it's dark, so the half moon glows bright in the sky, and I yawn, feelin' tired after all.

"Thank you," murmurs Victoria, as Ma starts gettin' her ready to sleep. "I like your story – tomorrow I'd like you to read me more."

When morning comes, I rub my wakin' eyes, sore from tryin' to read by candlelight in the garret, and glance out at the gloomy day.

Ma calls, "Hurry, Jacob. There's work to be done."

I land at the table, shovin' the wrinkled-up black shirt into my pants, wishin' our period of mournin' could keep me out of the hardware store a few more days.

Mr Cooper sits down to breakfast and says, "I'm opening the store today. You've stock-sorting to finish, Jacob."

And so I do.

When the church bells toll noon, he comes to the back and says, his voice stiff as iron, "You're free to go home, Jacob. I'll do the stock-sorting myself."

"But ... " I begin, wonderin' what I done wrong.

He says, "Tell your ma not to wait supper. I'll eat whenever I get there."

I shrug and trudge through a store that's empty and quiet, wonderin' if the reason nobody's here is the same one that kept folks from shakin' Mr Cooper's hand at the funeral yesterday. Everybody stayed back, like they were afraid that whatever Lizzy had might be catchin' from us.

Outside, the sun's streamin' through the puffy clouds and shinin' hot on Banker Anderson's shiny Model T – the only car for miles around. Dust's coverin' the long black body, but the headlamp trim's shinin' like pure gold.

Inside the car there's levers beside the steerin' wheel and more levers on the floor. I imagine climbin' onto that big front seat, and clutchin' the steerin' wheel in my hands, but, before I can, Mr Anderson comes out of Mrs Pendleton's shop, a big brown cardboard hatbox in his hands.

Ladies are always comin' from Dawson for the Widow Pendleton's hats – the banker must be gettin' a gift for his missus or somethin'.

So, Mr Anderson walks right past me, puts

the box in his car, sets some levers, then gets back out and sticks a crank in the engine. Crack!

I clamp my hands over my ears, lookin' around to see who's shootin, but figure out it's the car.

Mr Anderson adjusts the levers some more and tries the crank again. This time the engine starts. In a shake he's sittin' on that car seat, his feet pushin' pedals to make it go. It putts out into the street, spittin' smelly fumes out the back, followin' the wagon trail over to Dawson, where the banker lives.

It seems to me Dr Oliver's needin' a car more than Banker Anderson. Maybe if he had one, he could have come and saved our Lizzy with all his book learnin' from London.

Two ideas pop into my head for spendin' my time – the book, and Mr Higgins' horses grazin' in the meadow.

My feet start racin' through the dust, past the livery stable, past the town well. Soon, I'm climbin' between the two strands of barbed-wire fence, makin' sure not to snag the cloth of my shirt.

The meadow grass is crunchy, turnin' gold

and gettin' dry, but the horses chomp it just the same. I'm glad there's green trees scattered here and it's not flat and baked like in the book, where Dorothy comes from. I roll my lips under, stickin' both pointer fingers in my mouth and pullin' back my tongue, then let loose with the biggest, loudest whistle ever.

Mr Higgins' stallion stops grazin' on the grass. The two black mares stop scratchin' one another's backs with their teeth. And the foals stop chasin' each other round an old plough left sittin'.

The stallion runs, thunderin' over the ground, reachin' me first. His nose, where I rub it, is soft like the velveteen vest we buried Pa in. I drink in the horsey smell of the stallion, feelin' like I'm standin' here with Pa, talkin' about gettin' Ma to cure a foal with the colic.

Seems funny how animal-sick and people-sick is pretty much the same. Ma's been nursin' babies with the colic for as long as I remember, and she fixed Pa's foals up, too.

The bay filly nudges me in the arm, tryin' to get my attention, until the mare with a star in her forehead whinnies, callin' it back to her.

"Sure wish I could do whatever I want to,

like you can," I say to the stallion, combin' my fingers through his tangled black mane. But, soon as the words are out, I'm thinkin', what *do* I want to do?

Some thinkin' goes nowhere, so I get back to runnin' my fingers through his forelock, glad he's not head shy.

It's long past mealtime when I get home, but I'm starvin'. "Ma," I call, "what's to eat?"

Ma comes out of the bedroom, her face as grey as her eyes. "What happened? Why are you here?"

I can imagine she's thinkin' Mr Cooper told me to leave – he did, of course, but not for what she's worryin' about. Or else she's thinking that Mr Cooper's hurt or sick, which may be so, but I don't think she can fix up heart-sick.

"There's no folks in the store, so Mr Cooper gave me time off, Ma." I grin. "I can read more of the book to Victoria."

A sigh squeezes out of Ma. She says, "Torrie's asleep now. Didn't you eat the lunch I sent this morning?"

Shakin' my head, I explain, "No, I left when the church bells rang noon, but come back through Mr Higgins' horse pasture."

That gets a smile from her. She shakes her head and says, "You sure do love them horses, don't you? Just like your pa."

"But you're the healer, Ma, even with Pa's horses," I say, openin' the biscuit tin and pullin' out one made of dark, sweet molasses.

Sadness crosses Ma's face. "I couldn't help Lizzy, and Torrie's pa won't let me do anything for her, neither. I have to do what the doctor tells us."

I've been thinkin' about that. "You sure the doctor's wrong, Ma?" I ask.

She nods. "Muscles crampin' up need to be rubbed for pain, not wrapped up tight like you stop a cut from bleedin'. Makes no sense at all."

Puttin' it that way, I have to agree – I think about Pa's horses and wonder why the doctor can't see it for himself with all his learnin'.

I reach for another biscuit, but Ma pushes away my hand like she used to and says, "Bread and cheese first, so you leave the biscuits for later."

Chapter Six

For a second, it seems like the old Ma is back, the one who's really listenin' when I'm talkin'. But then she adds, "I hope that book helps your readin', so you can do more things in the store. You can't run it until you know numbers and words good."

I sigh. Runnin' the hardware store is the last thing I'm wantin' to do.

Once Victoria's awake, I'm ready to get back to readin'. "Do you want your medicine first?" I ask when she pulls the ryegrass straw from the empty cup.

She shakes her head. "No, it's awful. Just fills my head with fog. My legs still ache and ache."

"Oh," I say, lookin' at them wrapped up tight, lyin' still under Ma's old patchwork quilt. I tell her, "One time Red, Pa's best racin' horse, hurt a front leg so it was all tight-like and he couldn't use it – same as your infantile paralysis. Pa gentled Red down, but it took Ma to come up with how to heal him. Every day she worked his legs, stretchin' and rubbin' them, until the stallion healed up."

"I'm not a horse," Victoria says, and quickly adds, "I saw you with Mr Higgins' stallion again."

I think I hear longin' in her voice, and think how awful I'd feel lyin' on a sofa in front of the window, just watchin'. "He runs like he's a king, doesn't he? Proud."

"I'm beginning to think that running any way would be good." She smiles, but there's fear in her eyes. Fear of never runnin' again, I expect.

Then I think how I can still run, even though I have to spend my days in Mr Cooper's hardware store, and I don't feel so bad.

Before Victoria says anything else I open the book and start workin' on the words. I begin, *"Then a strange thing happened,"* and pretty soon I'm right there, flyin' high with Toto through the cyclone. How lucky Dorothy is to leave ugly, grey Kansas behind and end up with green trees, bright flowers, rare birds, a sparklin' brook …

I read the words of the old lady she meets: *"'You are welcome, most noble'…* what's S-o-r-c-e-r-e-s-s spell, Victoria?"

"Sorceress," she says.

I start again, near as shocked as Dorothy. *"'You are welcome, most noble Sorceress, to the land of the Munchkins. We are so grateful to you for having killed the Wicked Witch of the East, and for setting our people free from bondage.'"*

I read on and on, stoppin' only to get us tea with lemon to drink.

I just finish the part about Dorothy gettin' the silver shoes that belonged to the Wicked Witch of the East when Ma comes to see if Victoria needs anything. She does, and I go outside to wait while Ma takes care of it.

Even though my eyes are starin' across at the bay stallion, my head's whirlin' away in Oz, wonderin' how the witches and Munchkins can help Dorothy get home to Kansas – and why she'd be wantin' to go anyway. Surely Oz, with all its magic, must be a better place to be.

CHAPTER 7
Victoria

Papa disappears into the sunshine, without Jacob, without goodbye. Perhaps memory doesn't haunt him at the hardware store as it does me, here in our kitchen, where my sofa sits.

Jacob opens the book, his voice excited, like Elizabeth's was at story time, only he's the one reading, and I'm the one waiting.

I close my eyes, imagine a scarecrow, a creature stuffed with straw, so he has no brains at all – or so he thinks. Painted-on eyes wink at Dorothy, lips move, talk; stuffed overalls walk, even when the pole that holds them straight is gone.

Scarecrow doesn't mind his legs and arms and body being stuffed, because he can't feel anything at all, but I can. My fever's done, but the agony goes on. Spasms twist my legs, my feet, against the doctor's splints, and I long to be like Scarecrow. A head stuffed with straw seems not too dear a price to pay to lose this pain.

Crow tells Scarecrow, *"Brains are the only things worth having in this world, no matter whether one is a crow or a man."*

But what does Crow know? He has wings to fly and can't grasp how it feels to have legs that wither, shrivel, die.

Mother Alice, skin ivory white like the piano keys against her mourning dress, listens to Jacob reading for a while. She shakes her head. "What foolish things," she says with a laugh. "Imagine a scarecrow telling tales."

Jacob closes the book and says to her, "Tell us a tale, Ma, about learnin' nursin' back in England."

His eyes are serious, pleading, begging me to listen. So I do.

"Well," Mother Alice says, "the Sisters of Mercy cared for us, taught us the plants to use for healin'. I learned to help the poor beyond the convent walls, bein' but twelve when I first midwifed a babe and brought it cryin' into the world ..."

My legs throb, hamstring muscles tight,

tugging and tugging against the splints until my body screams back in pain.

"Mother Alice," I say, remembering the doctor's words, the wolfsbane, Papa's orders, "the doctor's medicine doesn't help. The tight wrapping doesn't help." My voice cracks; tears fill my eyes and run hot down my cheeks. I feel a fool, like Scarecrow, and wish I, too, had a brain to know what to choose.

"Let Ma help you," says Jacob, voice tight.

I nod, too tired to argue. Papa isn't here – doesn't know how I feel. Anything is better than this. I know Margaret would tell me to take a chance, grab on to hope, not lie here feeling sorry for myself.

Mother Alice stands, sets about her task. The wood-fired stove, its top polished glossy black, soon holds a crackling fire. Overtop, the yellow-fronted warming oven sits empty while steam rises out of the water reservoir on its side.

The room, already warm, grows hot. What will Papa say?

Mother Alice kneels and unwraps the binding around my feet, her story unravelling like the cloth and splints from my legs. "I once helped a child, not much more than a babe in arms. Her sickness was a little like yours. After a while she could stand and later on she walked." Mother Alice's eyes glow, the memory a gleam of pleasure on her face.

Through the window, I see Jacob at the woodpile, both hands on the axe high above his head. *Thwack!* The blade hits a log. *Thwack*, then *crack*, *crack* as the log splits and woodchips fly.

He pushes through the door, arms full, and drops the pieces, *thud*, into the woodbox beside the stove.

Mother Alice lifts the cast-iron skillet, shakes it, pours hot white salt into a small sugar bag. "Which leg hurts more?" she asks, standing over me.

I'm half afraid to answer, so I point, and she lays the bag in place. While it cools, her keen eyes watch me, my face, my leg. The bag feels hot, like sand in the sun, nothing more.

Jacob sighs.

Mother Alice says, "Linseed meal poultice may work." She holds a single finger to her lip and chin, as if to shush her own thinking. "It draws a boil, soothes a skin ulcer."

I watch them work – mother and son – their movements smooth, practised, words no more useful than sheet music to a songbird.

The linseed meal, when Mother Alice brings it, is a burden on my leg. "No," I gasp, grasping its soft, mushy weight between my fingers, pushing it from my skin. "It's too heavy – it makes the pain even worse," I whimper, a child having a tantrum.

"Then we'll make it light," says Mother Alice. "Jacob, fetch the old wool blanket from the bag upstairs."

She hastens to the stove again and puts the kettle on to boil. For tea, I think, and close my eyes against the pain.

Jacob's feet meet the floor – thump, thump – beneath the garret ladder. "What now?" he asks, tendrils of cream-coloured blanket snaking behind him.

"Tear it into strips," Mother Alice says, liquid splashing into a pan. "We'll start with two."

The sound of ripping cloth is sharp. Splat. It hits the water.

Mother Alice brings the pan, water sloshing over its sides, towards me, drops on her knees, sets it beside my feet. "This has to be hot," she says, a question in her eyes.

"If it takes away the pain ..." I start, then stop, waiting as the odour of hot wool fills my nostrils.

The first wool strip touches my legs and burns like a log pulled from orange, licking flames and held against them. I scream – a hollow sound – and pound my arms against the pillows, wishing for courage like the cowardly lion.

Mother Alice lifts, wraps, lifts, wraps.

I bite my lip and pummel feathers.

Jacob dips his hands, red like fire, into the steaming pan, wrings out the wide cream ribbon and passes it to Mother Alice.

Muscles relax.

For the first time in a week I feel no pain, even as the hot packs cool against my skin. "Again," I say, anxious for more.

At night, when Papa comes, my legs are safe beneath the quilt, wrapped loose in case he cares to look. But he doesn't. His sky-blue eyes are far away, empty of clouds, of twinkling stars, of hope.

We try, the three of us, to cover our deceit.

Shepherd's pie, Papa's favourite, sits steaming on the table, mashed potato crust brown and crispy.

Jacob's shirt is done up proper and Mother Alice's hair is twisted into a knot that falls down her back, her cheeks rosy from the heat. Not that Papa sees.

But we know, and smile.

"Will you need me tomorrow?" Jacob asks. Lemon pudding drips from his spoon, missing his shirt, and onto the white porcelain plate.

Papa shakes his head, his hair greyer than it was before the infantile paralysis, before Elizabeth died. "No," he says, his voice heavy.

We read again, Jacob and I, Oz dragging us in, as if we're two against four in a tug-of-war.

Scarecrow says, "*It must be inconvenient to be made of flesh,*" and I sigh, pain creeping into mine once more.

Dorothy finds Tin Woodman, his joints rusted and needing oil, and Jacob's eyes raise as he reads, "'*I might have stood there always, if you had not come along.*'"

I nod, thinking of the hot wool rags — my tin of oil.

Chapter Seven

Tin Woodman joins the quest to Oz. Having neither brain nor heart, he yearns for the love he's lost, for the happiness he says, *"is the best thing in the world"* – and he needs a heart for that.

Jacob's voice creaks at last – tired, worn – and he closes the cover on Oz. If only Margaret was here. She could take a turn reading when Jacob's done and spend these nights with us.

"It's time, Torrie," Mother Alice says, her eyes caring, face firm, "for a proper night, in bed."

I screech, "I can't! I can't sleep there ... not yet."

Papa comes, picks me up like I'm a sack of flour, and says, "Victoria, it's time. Your sister's gone."

I turn my face to his chest and listen to his heart thump. Then, when the bedroom door squeaks open, it flutters and stops as he stares at the bed.

My tears wet his shirt sleeves.

Mother Alice turns back the bedcover, opens the window. Papa lays me on the bed. "Good night," he whispers, as my back touches the crisp sheet and sinks in to the soft mattress.

The wicker carriage of dolls – Elizabeth's and

mine – sits against one wall. Everything else of hers is gone. Her dresses. Her toys. Her smell. Her giggles. Her soft, warm body.

I cry.

Mother Alice, eyes sad, settles me in for the night and whispers, "We all miss her."

I lie awake, listen to a chorus of crickets, watch a shooting star fall from the sky and disappear before I can make a wish.

The days melt into one another, each crimson sunset followed by a golden sunrise. Sam from next door passes on his way to the livery, eyes straight ahead, whistling a Pied Piper tune that's lured all the children away, leaving me to drown alone in loneliness, without Margaret to play with. Little Will waves and I wave back, smiling until his mama pulls him through the door. They're all afraid of me, of the infantile paralysis, like the Cowardly Lion in Oz, but, as the lion says, *"That doesn't make me any braver."*

In the evenings, Papa comes home and asks, "Are you better, Torrie?"

I answer, "Yes, I am," but he's not listening for the answer. Instead, he picks up the paper and hides behind its pages.

Chapter Seven

In the silence of the day, Mother Alice and Jacob take turns at heating the water, dipping the wool cloths, wrapping them around my legs, waiting for them to cool, then doing it all again.

Mother Alice's long, thin fingers run down my legs, stretch the hamstring muscles, knead the knots of twisted flesh. She holds my heel in the cup of one hand, the underside of my knee in the other, then works my leg to take steps in the air.

I giggle. "Jacob," I say. "Guess I'm like your pa's horse after all." My leg works up and down, back and forth.

"I'm hopin' you win the race," he says, his rag twisting between his hands, the water dripping, splashing into the pan.

"Me, too," I say, although I feel more like Dorothy and her company on the way to Oz, standing at the edge of a very wide ditch, deep and full of big, jagged rocks, with sides so steep none can climb down. And, like the Cowardly Lion, *"I am terribly afraid of falling."*

CHAPTER 8 JACOB

This mornin' Ma wrapped Victoria's legs back up so tight I thought they'd choke, ready for me to bring the doctor back. Mr Cooper ordered it, to make sure she's doin' all right. Too bad he couldn't open his eyes for a look instead.

Dr Oliver never guessed at nothin', just told Mr Cooper to start lookin' for a wheelchair, since those afflicted with infantile paralysis never walk again. I couldn't look at Victoria then, knowin' how bad that'd make me feel, so I watched her pa instead. He never flinched, not a bit, just thanked the doctor for his time and sent me to drive him back to Dawson.

The doctor, he was even friendly to Ma, tellin' her how good Victoria looks with her nursin', like he was sorry about sayin' that using wolfsbane was witchery.

Chapter Eight

Up front, the stallion – Mr Higgins told me this morning his name's Duke – is prancin' right along, pullin' the buggy as easy as me and Ma pull sticky toffee, even though it's his second time up the road today.

Dr Oliver leans back, lights up his pipe and says, "So, Jacob, how old are you?"

"Fifteen," I answer, thinkin' how my birthday's comin' up soon – last day next month – and Ma's sure to make me a chocolate cake, since she can cook whatever she wants with Mr Cooper buyin' the food.

"And what are you aiming to do with your life, Jacob?" he asks, blowing out a big ring of cherry-smellin' smoke.

I open my mouth to say "farmin'", but close it quick. "Well, Ma's hopin' I'll stay on workin' in the store with Mr Cooper."

The doctor smiles. "I'm sure that's a good idea, since he has no son of his own to take over."

I nod back, not answerin' cause a lump the size of a dumplin' sticks itself in my throat.

"But what about you, Jacob? Do you enjoy storekeeping?" he says, like he's tryin' to be friends.

The smell of a green-covered pond drifts up,

along with a swarm of mozzies that make Duke shake his head. I slap one that lands on my shirt, squishin' it. The doctor looks at me again and I try to figure out how to answer his question.

"Well," I start, "I like sortin' the stuff I know and helpin' find things, so that part's all right. My readin' and numbers aren't too good, since Teacher put me out of school when I was just past twelve. But Victoria, she's helpin' me remember what I learned then, and teachin' me more."

The doctor turns to me, a little teasin' grin on his face. "So, what got you put out of school, young man? Were you playing tricks on the teacher?"

About there my face feels warm and I'm mad right off, so I start to spill the story even Ma don't know, of how Freddie Thornhill got me thrown out of school.

"No, sir," I say, "I never played tricks on nobody. It was all because I punched Freddie in the nose – knocked him cold and made my knuckles bleed, turn black and blue and swell."

Wriggling on his seat, like he's afraid I'll punch him next, Dr Oliver says, "Why did you punch Freddie in the nose?"

Funny how he's the first to ask. Teacher didn't.

Ma didn't. Even Freddie's pa didn't, when he came to get Ma to midwife for his missus.

"Well," I say, "it was all because of Freddie's big mouth. Ma told you how Sister Mary taught her about herbs and stuff, back in England, and she's been fixin' coughs and boils and broken bones and sores and birthin' babies since before she came here. Kind of like you."

When I turn to look in his face, all he does is clear his throat, like he's thinkin' the same as Freddie – that fixin' people don't make Ma a nurse at all, even after what he said today.

But I go on. "About two days before, Freddie's Grandpa Jake came to Ma with a big sore on his foot, all festered and lookin' green. Ma took one look and said he'd left it too long and would have to get on over to Dawson, get it amputated by the doctor, 'cos it had turned gangrene. Of course, he was havin' none of that and said Ma wasn't a nurse at all, just a witch handin' out potions. Next day his grandpa died and Freddie said Ma had put a spell on his grandpa that killed him, for tellin' her she wasn't a real nurse." This time I don't look at him, just spit a wad at the wooden floor of the buggy, waitin' for what he has to say.

"I'm sure your ma was right and Freddie's grandpa needed a doctor. She didn't kill him, since you can't put a spell on somebody," he says, still pretty friendly, but then his voice grows cold as well water on a hot summer day. "Freddie's grandpa should have gone to the doctor right off, not somebody practising medicine without proper training."

My mouth drops open and I swallow a mozzie.

Right then, I decide Victoria's going to walk again, and that I'm going to help her do it, just to prove a person needs more than medical school to be a healer. Ma saw right through Dr Oliver's treatment, how it was hurtin' Victoria even more, and she eased her pain right away with the heat and rubbin' the muscles. I'm bettin' if we keep workin' Victoria's legs, she'll run again, just like Pa's horse, instead of needin' the wheelchair the doctor's ordered.

"I'm sure Ma was right," I say, keepin' my eyes on Duke's feet, feelin' my anger with each clip-clop and puff of dust.

The doctor tips up his pipe, knocks out the tobacco and drops it back in his black bag, then pulls his cap over his eyes, pretendin' to be sleepy again. It seems to me, watchin' him out of the corner of my eye, that Scarecrow could be right. If the doctor had brains, he should be able to use them and know in his heart that any thinking person should help somebody who's suffering, if they can – no matter if they're school-trained or not.

Next morning, Mr Cooper says between a mouthful of eggs and one of toast, "I need you at the hardware store, Jacob."

"Yes, sir," I answer quick, my day bust up like one of the eggshells lyin' in pieces beside the frypan.

Ma glances at me, a warnin' in her eyes tellin' me I'd best be quiet and do as I'm told. "People are comin' in now?" she asks. "They're not afraid of …"

Inside my head, I add: of the disease that took Lizzy and left Victoria lyin' in bed.

Mr Cooper says, "Business is fine. Things were just slow for the hot weather."

"Oh," Ma says, "that's good."

Everywhere I look around the kitchen I can still see Lizzy walkin', talkin', playin' with her dolly – everywhere but in Mr Cooper's eyes. She's gone from there.

It seems strange to take the sack of lunch and head to the store. The Widow Pendleton greets me like I was here yesterday, saying, "Good mornin', Jacob. Is your Uncle Charlie done haying?"

"Haven't seen him in a while," I say, feeling guilty because I haven't even thought about him much. All my time's been taken up with Oz and helping Victoria use her legs again.

Inside, the hardware store is tidy – not one hammer or nail seems out of place. What can there be for me to do?

Mr Cooper pulls the accounts books from under the counter. "You'll run the cash register while I do accounts today," he says, settling down on the three-legged stool.

Before I've even got around the counter, Mrs Hillman hurries in, the big flowers on her hat floppin' back and forth, like they're blowin' in the wind, as she nods, pickin' through the knives in the drawer I open for her.

She holds up one with a carved horn handle

and asks, "Is this a good-quality blade? I don't want to be paying for just a pretty handle."

I heft the knife in my hand, tryin' it for balance. "I'd say it's a good one, ma'am," I answer.

One after another she goes through the knives, while I stand, waiting. This one has too long a blade, that one too short. This one is too heavy, that one too light. Finally, she picks up the first knife again, and says, "I'll take this one."

Mr Cooper doesn't say anythin', but I know he's watchin' my every move as I round the counter, step up to the register and study the row of round, numbered silver keys. My heart's poundin' like I'm runnin' after Duke in the pasture instead of him comin' to me when I whistle.

"Would you like me to wrap that up for you, Mrs Hillman," I ask, holding out my hand.

"Certainly," she says, soundin' like she thinks I should have known what she wanted, "and put it on my account."

My hand shakes as I rip a long piece of paper off the roll, wrap the knife in it, tie it off with string and hand it to Mrs Hillman. My finger hits one key on the register, then another. Ching, ching. That done, I turn and look at Mr Cooper, feelin' nervous as a newly-trained colt. Does he want me to enter the numbers in the ledger or will he?

He pushes the book at me. "Accounts Payable" it says. Guess I'm supposed to enter the figures. The yellow pencil trembles in my hand – I'll be makin' wavy lines, not numbers, if I'm not careful. So I tighten up my grip, flip open the ledger and write the numbers, neat and square.

When Mrs Hillman leaves, Mr Cooper doesn't say anything, just keeps totallin' columns and writin' in the book.

It seems every person in town needs some kind of hardware this morning. I dig for bolts and count out nails. I pull out one can of distemper paint. I even climb up the ladder to bring down a dusty lantern that must have been hangin' there a year or more.

Each ching, ching of the cash register makes me mad as a wet hen. What am I doin' inside this stuffy old store, wipin' dust off shelves and pokin' at silver keys on a cash register?

My head keeps wandering away from what I'm doing to the great Wizard of Oz, wondering what he might really be like. The story says some think he looks like an elephant, a bird, a cat, a fairy, a brownie, or whatever pleases him. I'm not sure what I'd be if I could be anything. When I first came here, I'd have picked Mr Higgins' stallion, runnin' free through the meadow.

Now, since Lizzy's died and Victoria has the paralysis, I'm thinking there must be something else that would be better. One thing I know for sure, I'd like to find the yellow brick road and follow it into the Emerald City, with its great high thick green walls and the gate all studded with sparkling emeralds. I'd push that bell in a second and walk into the high-arched room, and then … Well, then I would have to want something that wasn't idle or foolish, so the wizard didn't destroy me in a second. I'm wondering if wanting a brain, a heart and courage will be good enough for the wizard. And what of Kansas? Can the wizard get Dorothy back to Kansas?

Can I ever get back to the farm?

The noon church bell hasn't even rung when old Percy totters in, restin' his wrinkled hand on the counter. I wonder what he's buildin' today.

Percy glances around the store, takin' in Mr Cooper sittin' at his ledgers, and says, "Son, how much you know 'bout cabinetmaking?"

I look back at Mr Cooper, wishin' he'd step up to the counter and let me go. But his hand is movin' across the paper and he's not lookin' back at me. So I say, "Not very much yet, sir."

Percy's face wrinkles up even more. He says, "Son, you hafta know what folks is lookin' for to be in hardware."

I'm hot and I'm thirsty and I'm tired, so before I can bite back the words they fall out. "I'm a farmer and I know lots about farmin'."

"What 'bout cabinets?" he says.

"Not much." I feel like I'm a calf strugglin' backwards through the mud, gettin' caught up in my own words.

"Well, son," he says, "I can help you with that, I sure can."

Last thing I want is help from an old man who spends his days whittlin' scraps of wood to stick on bigger scraps of wood. I glance at Mr Cooper, tryin' to measure out my words so they don't make him too mad. "I'm kind of busy today, sir, so, if I can just help you find what you're lookin' for, that would be good."

"I'm not looking fer much," he says. "Drawer

I'm makin' uses a sliding dovetail and I been doing that for close t' fifty years."

Old Percy's eyes are tellin' me this is where I'm supposed to ask what a slidin' dovetail is, and start my learnin', but I can't. It's kind of like readin' – until I found a book that looked interestin', there didn't seem to be much point in studyin' at all those letters lyin' there on the paper. And, right about now, there doesn't seem to be much point in figurin' out how to use all these things in the hardware store.

When I glance back at Mr Cooper, his eyes are tellin' me the same thing as old Percy's. I don't need proddin' to hear Ma's voice inside my head, sayin' this is the best future for me, and just to do what needs doin'. And Pa – well, Uncle Charlie's told me often enough about how Pa never meant to be a dirt farmer at all, but wanted to be a farrier or veterinarian. He only stayed farming 'cos his pa made him promise when he died.

But nobody made me promise anything, not even Ma.

I straighten my shoulders and say to old Percy, "It's about time to make a pot of tea. Would you be wantin' a cup?"

CHAPTER 9
Victoria

A fly buzzes in the silent room. I'm alone. Jacob is at the hardware store with Pa, Mother Alice outside in the garden.

What am I to do? Lie here and wait for the wheelchair the doctor ordered? Wait for somebody to lift me into it? Wait for Margaret to come home to push me around?

It's hot and I lie uncovered, white cotton night-gown up over knees that grow knobblier each day. Lying here, propped up with pillows, I feel like a babe in a cradle with nothing to do but sing myself a lullaby. I miss summer – gathering wild berries, playing tag in the dark, beating Margaret at hopscotch …

Perhaps I'll lie here forever, watching my legs shrivel and hang useless, like the doctor says. I think of Queen Victoria, the longest-reigning

British monarch, and sigh. She ruled a nation for sixty-three years – right hand holding her sceptre, left, the orb.

She came into the world on the twenty-fourth of May – as did I. She used her left hand to eat, to write, to do needlework – as do I. She studied languages, music, mathematics, and history – as did I.

I turn my hands to inspect my skin, now grown smooth with laziness, and wonder what of the sceptre that should have been mine – the wooden ruler of the classroom, the kingdom I've worked to earn.

The fly zips through the kitchen, buzzes over a loaf of bread, then lands on the window pane above my head. I swat. Arms flapping and hands slapping, I scare him from the sunshine outside.

He lands. Settles on my toe. Tickles my skin.

I lean down. Swat.

He prances over my toe, wings wiggling, as if he's dancing on my grave.

That makes angry and I suck a great big breath and stare at my toe, glaring at the winged demon.

My toe moves.

The fly buzzes away.

"Mother Alice," I shout. "Mother Alice, come quick!"

The screen door slams and Mother Alice appears, breathless, wisps of hair falling over her cheeks. "What is it, Torrie? What's ailin' you?"

I point and wiggle my toes a tiny bit again. "They move, Mother Alice, they move."

She drops the handful of potatoes on the table, crosses the room in three long strides, then drops down on the floor. "You can do this, Torrie," she says, her grey eyes strong as steel. "You can make them work again."

Later, while she wraps my legs with hot wool, filling the room with the smell I've come to love, we talk, just she and I, about things long past.

"I remember the letter," she says. "The one Jacob's pa wrote askin' me to leave the orphanage, be his wife, after I put my name in to be a mail-order bride. I didn't take to readin' as a child, you see. The letters all squiggled across the page, makin' no sense at all, so Sister Mary had to read it to me. And Sister Mary, dear Sister Mary, said his offer was most kind and his words came out soundin' like he be an honest man. I could have took the veil, but, even though I liked nursin' the poor, the church was not my callin'."

Mother Alice stops talking and bends, dipping her hands in the steaming water. She wrings out another wool rag and wraps it around my other leg. How strange that her hands have the gift to heal while her brain can't figure out the way to read.

Thinking of reading makes me remember Elizabeth, nestled in my lap, finger in my book, following along while I read. "I miss her, little Elizabeth," I say. "Poor baby, she'll never get her first day of school ..."

My voice chokes as a horse trots by outside the window, pulling a buggy as big and black as the hearse that carried her away.

"Her eyes sparkled like them green emeralds in your Oz book," Mother Alice goes on. "Every time you read her a story, Lizzy'd say to me after, 'Soon I'll know what letters mean and I'll read every book in the world to you.'" She wipes her eyes, sniffs a bit, and tries to hide her sorrow.

Then she works my legs harder so they tingle – a good tingle, not bad, and I wiggle my toes again, just to see them move.

"I'm ready for school, for Margaret to be back home again from her aunt's," I say.

"She's your friend, Margaret Lowsley?"

I sigh, feeling selfish, and say, "Since first day of school. She's been gone since you came, helping her aunt with twin baby boys."

Mother Alice smiles. "I had a friend once."

"What was she like?" I ask. I can't imagine Mother Alice whispering with a friend, sharing secrets, giggling.

"Well," says Mother Alice, "she'd blue eyes like yours, and her name was Victoria, too. She come to the orphanage when she was nine, her family lost to sickness. We was friends for seven years, until I left."

I ask slowly, "You called her Torrie, didn't you?" Her nod fills me with knowing.

She says, "Torrie when we were children, Victoria when we were grown women and, finally, Sister Victoria when she took the veil."

The afternoon passes – shared words float me downstream, visiting places I've never been.

"Will you … tell your pa?" Mother Alice asks, rising when she's done my legs.

I think of the doctor calling the wolfsbane

witchery, and Papa, stern-faced, watching my legs swallowed up as I screamed in pain. His words were clear – follow the doctor's orders. Yesterday he stayed away while the doctor was here, tending the hardware, tending the store, leaving me for someone else to tend.

"No," I whisper. "Not yet. I won't tell him yet." I have a brain to make my own choice, a heart to know who to trust, and courage to see this through.

While Mother Alice starts supper, I pick up the book and it falls open on the great and the terrible Wizard of Oz telling Dorothy, *"In this country everyone must pay for everything he gets."*

I wonder what I must pay to run again.

Jacob comes home, and Mother Alice stands in the kitchen, mixing bread pudding full of juicy raisins, Papa's favourite dessert. She asks him, "Are you alone?"

He nods. "Mr Cooper, he's finished accounts, so sent me on early."

"That's good," I call. "Come see what I can do!" Then I tug back the quilt, uncover my legs and wiggle my toes.

A smile grabs his face, parts his lips, lights up his eyes and puts a dimple in his chin. "They're movin'!" he says. "Pretty soon feet, then legs!"

I nod, too excited to talk.

He kneels down by the sofa and puts warm hands against my heels. "Push," he says. "Push against my hand."

I will my legs to move, lift up, have life again, but my strength is gone, flown away like Dorothy to Oz.

"Try again," he says and grins when nothing happens. "Guess they need a rest. Tomorrow we'll do it again."

The crickets are chirping when Papa comes home. There's a fine golden-wood chair with a wheel on each leg in his hands. He grabs me up, wrapped in my quilt, and sets me between the wooden arms.

"Did old Percy build that?" Jacob asks.

Papa nods. "Yes, he did."

"Tell him thank you, Papa," I say, as he pushes me, wheels squeaking, across the floor. "And thank you, too."

My heart has wings, sings like a choir of angels.

Chapter Nine

"Now you can sit to the table," says Mother Alice, filling plates. "It will feel like …"

We're a family again, I think, my arms resting on the oilcloth, my eyes drinking in the sight of Papa sitting across the table.

Before I can speak, Papa glances from me to Mother Alice and says, "The chair will make less work."

His words, cold and sharp as hailstones hurled out of the sky on a hot summer's day, bring tears to my eyes. Papa has become like Tin Woodman.

Each day, through the window, I watch Jacob run, chase butterflies across the meadow, throw his arms around the stallion's neck, rub the soft, downy noses of the foals.

Papa doesn't see Jacob, or me …

Oz, the great and terrible, sets Dorothy to a ghastly task – kill the Wicked Witch of the West – a task as out of reach as mine, of running again. But Dorothy has Scarecrow, Tin Woodman and Cowardly Lion for help. And I have Jacob and Mother Alice.

I mark Xs on the calendar, waiting for Margaret to come home before summer ends, and school to begin again.

Each night, Jacob and I read, sometimes him to me, sometimes me to him. We reach the part where *"The Wicked Witch laughed to herself, and thought, 'I can still make Dorothy my slave, for she does not know how to use her power.'"*

Jacob whispers to me, "You have power, too, Victoria."

"I need the silver shoes," I say, only half in jest. "Then I'd be sure that some day I'd run again."

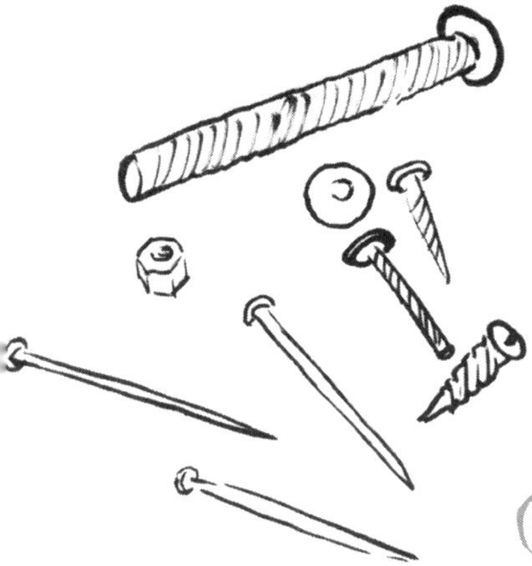

CHAPTER 10 JACOB

When night comes again, I open the book, sayin' to Victoria, "It sure enough was awful to find, when Dorothy melted the Wicked Witch of the West, that the Wizard of Oz really had no powers at all. How will she get home to Kansas? How will Scarecrow, Tin Woodman and Cowardly Lion get their wishes?"

Victoria's eyes watch her pa as she says, "I guess sometimes wishes aren't meant to be."

I figure she's rememberin' how he used to laugh at nights, tease little Lizzy, toss jacks, tell stories about England, where he was born, same as Ma. Now he sits sad and quiet, like a lion without its roar.

Turns out, though, that Oz, even though he's not much at bein' a wizard, is a pretty good man.

He tells Scarecrow he doesn't need brains, since he's learning something every day, like a baby growing or me with readin', and experience is the only thing that brings knowledge. I guess I've figured that out some, since I spent all that time spelling out words in school, just to discover they were easier to learn when they were put together in a story I wanted to know.

He tells Tin Woodman that he's wrong to want a heart, for *"it makes most people unhappy."* And I think of little Lizzy, gone, and know it wouldn't hurt if I didn't have a heart. And maybe, if I didn't have a heart that wasn't in hardware, I could be happy doing whatever Ma wanted, so that's hurtin' me, too.

And he tells Cowardly Lion he has plenty of courage, so all he needs is confidence in himself – *"True courage is in facing danger when you are afraid."* I imagine Ma was afraid, leavin' the farm and marrying up with Victoria's pa, and Victoria sure enough is afraid she'll never walk or run again. And me, I'm sure enough afraid I'll spend my whole life doin' something I hate.

Truth be told, in my opinion Scarecrow really was thoughtful, Tin Woodman cared about others, so he had a heart, and Cowardly Lion was very brave when he had to be. So they had what they wanted inside of themselves all along, anyway. Now I can't help but wonder what I want, and if it's been inside of me all along, too.

But Dorothy's problem of getting home to Kansas – well, home just isn't something you can keep inside yourself and pull out when you need it, any more than I can just get back to the farm.

At daybreak I wake to a crow's caw, wishin' it was a rooster's crow instead. One corner of the garret holds my straw-stuffed mattress on the floor, my small pile of clothes and Pa's hand-tooled saddle – the only thing of his I brought along, besides his prize razor. I left all the tools for cleaning and trimming horses' hooves for Uncle Charlie on the farm.

I pull on my shirt, tighten up my collar, stare in the little brown, framed mirror Ma hung for me, and see a lot more brown hairs on my chin than the first time I tried out that razor.

Downstairs, Ma's fixing breakfast, same as usual. Victoria's sitting at the table, next to her pa. Nothing looks a lot different than when Ma and me moved here, even though nothing's the same at all.

"Good morning, Jacob," says Victoria, eyes glowing. "Today you'll get to meet Margaret."

Ma nods. "It's good to see you all excited, Torrie."

Victoria's pa sets down his tea, stares across the table. "Margaret's mother will bring her over soon as she arrives," he says. "She'll tell her about your … condition before they come."

I've been wishin' for the past few weeks we'd told Victoria's pa that she wasn't following the doctor's orders at all, but was healin' up good with Ma's nursin'. It doesn't seem fair him believin' she's going to be in a wheelchair for good when she's able to move her feet and legs.

Victoria seems to be thinking the same thing, and she says, "Papa, I can … get better, you know."

But he doesn't answer, and the other three of us all glance at one another and let it slide again.

The weather's changin', coolin' off some, so I can smell harvest on the wind as we walk to the hardware store. Back home, Uncle Charlie will be done puttin′ up the hay with the Clydesdale horses, ready to start harvestin′ the grain. I′ll miss threshin′ with all the neighbours, once all the wheat is dried out.

Eloise Jarvis has started working for the Widow Pendleton, so the first thing I do at the store is grab a broom to sweep off the sidewalk, hopin′ she comes out to do the same. Sure enough, there she is right after me, auburn hair pulled up on top, covered by a wide-brimmed yellow hat.

"Good morning, Jacob," she says, a smile playin′ over her fine, even white teeth. "Nice day, isn′t it?"

Swish and some dust flies. "Sure is," I say. "Harvest is rolling around."

"School, too," she says, wrinkling up her little nose. "I sure am glad not to be going back to Mrs Needlemeyer′s class next week. She just about took all the fun there was in school right out."

Swish-swish and another little cloud of dust swirls up.

I′ve been thinking about school, too, though I don′t see it quite the way Eloise does. Guess that′s because it quit me, instead of me quittin′ it.

"So, you′re planning to stay on here at the

millinery?" I ask.

She does a little sashay on the sidewalk, swirling her blue skirt like she's ready for a barn dance.

"Sure am," she says. "Sixteen's well past old enough for finishin' school." Then she puffs out a little with pride and adds, "Hat I made last week sold for top price yesterday, to the druggist's wife from Dawson. She said she hadn't ever seen anything prettier."

By now both of us are leaning on our brooms so, when Mr Cooper sticks his head out, I say guiltily, "I have to get to work," and pull my broom through the door after me.

He doesn't say anything, just nods at the pile of screwdrivers and screws I've been sorting out the back.

There's just too many things shootin' through my mind this morning for me to settle in to work easy. I wish my chores were in the back room, so I could sneak out and run through Mr Higgins' meadow, talk to the horses for a minute, but they aren't.

Instead, I'm sittin', lookin' at half a dozen different screws for wood and metal, all mixed together, all different sizes, wishing the world had stayed usin' flat, headless nails or that I wasn't workin' in a hardware store.

Mr Cooper checks in every half hour or so, telling me what all I've got mixed up and priced wrong. Each minute porin' over the pile when he's done makes me feel hotter and madder.

Gong, gong, gong, tolls the church bell.

My back hurts from bending over the little bins and I straighten, feeling like a convict that's been prayin' for forgiveness.

Before we stop for lunch, Mr Cooper goes through the bins I've done, checkin' one last time and shakin' his head.

His voice is grim – worse than Teacher's when I missed every word on the spelling test. "Jacob, you still aren't sorting the Phillips screws from these new Robinson screws."

I don't answer.

"Jacob, do you even look what you're doing?"

I get up, but still don't answer.

Mr Cooper stands, too, but now I realise I've grown a little taller, so his eyes are lower than mine. I stare down.

He says, "Jacob, you will work at this for as long as it takes to get it right."

I don't even stop to think, just turn, walk through the door and let it slam behind me, running smack into a fly that buzzes in my face. My feet clip-clop over the wood-slatted sidewalk, and I try to think. But I can't.

My feet start to run, flying past the houses, and I'm wishin' for a cyclone that would fly me to Oz, even if the Wizard doesn't really have any magic.

My heart pounds like my feet hittin' the ground, and each thump takes down a yellow flower or two on the hillside – squashes it flat. I can hardly breathe for being mad.

Finally, out of air, I flop under a tree. Two birds chirp at me, or maybe one another – I wish I'd said something to Mr Cooper before I ran off.

The foals wander up in a few minutes, nuzzling my hands with their noses. They don't care what I do durin' the day, long as I'm friendly when I get here. From this little rise I can see the main street of town, all the way to our house. As I watch, Eloise comes out of the Widow Pendleton's shop, carrying a hatbox for a lady twice as wide as her. The woman gets in a two-seater buggy and grabs the box up beside her.

Eloise is one of the prettiest girls in town.

Chapter Ten

It gets easier to think as I stare at the clouds, imagining them as Munchkins and wizards and other things nobody's ever seen.

In a while, a big bay stallion trots into town, pullin' a carriage up to the Lowsley house, and I remember that Margaret, Victoria's friend, is coming home today. A girl gets out, but all I can tell is that she's taller than her ma, and thin like a willow stick.

My stomach rumbles, remindin' me that I ran off before I ate the lunch Ma sent with us this morning to the store.

Before I get around to standing and heading home, I hear a car putt-putting down the road. Like I figure, it's the Banker Anderson's Model T. This time, though, there's three people get out at the millinery store – two men and a woman with a parasol over her head, for the sun.

Banker Anderson and the lady – his wife, I figure – go into the Widow Pendleton's shop. The other man starts walkin' down the street.

I stare for a while, tryin' to figure out where he's going. When I get it, I leap up and start running. He's the doctor! On his way to see Victoria.

I fly over the grass.

Wriggle through the fence.

Half run, half fall, down the hill.

Take the shortcut past the Madeleys' hedge. I have to warn Ma and Victoria. Give them time to get her legs wrapped up.

Pantin' like a horse that's run for miles, I pull up with a stitch in my side. The doctor's already at the front step, knockin' on the door.

Ma opens it and I'm close enough to see her face drop. She needs me, so I take another big gulp of air and run the rest of the way.

I push inside and stop.

"Where are the splints, the wraps for her legs?" says Dr Oliver, his voice half a shout.

Ma says, "They gave her pain, so we took them off."

He points at the wool rags and hot water. "What are you doing?"

"Puttin' on heat for the pain," Ma says, standing straight and starin' him in the eye.

"Let me … " Victoria begins, but, before she can finish, the doctor spins around and shoves past me at the door.

I'm left standing there like a fool, lookin' at their faces.

Chapter Ten

"Well, there's nothin' more to do," says Ma, then turns to me, a question on her face. "Jacob?"

She doesn't ask what happened, but I tell her anyway. "I walked out of the hardware store."

Ma drops the wool rag she's picked up, stomps her foot down hard and says, "Jacob, you get right back over there and back to work."

Victoria sits watchin' from her chair with wheels, a wrap on one leg, the other still lookin' too weak to hold up a sunflower, never mind a girl. She says, "What do you want to do, Jacob?"

My voice cracks when I answer, "I don't know. Eat, I guess."

Victoria grins. "Eat? It's long past lunch."

There's no smile on Ma's face, but she points at some rolls, smelling strong of cinnamon and dripping with melted sugar, coolin' on the table. In two steps I'm in front of them, breaking one away from the rest, taking a big sugary bite.

"Are they as good as they smell?" asks Victoria, stretching out her bare leg to be wrapped.

Instead of answering, I lick the cinnamon stickiness from my fingers and start another one.

I'm well into my third roll by the time Victoria's pa opens the door. The doctor's right behind him, their faces both scowling and angry.

"What's going on here?" demands Mr Cooper.

"I … " begins Victoria.

Her pa cuts her off, sayin', "You keep quiet, Victoria. I'm asking Alice what's going on."

Ma straightens her shoulders, faces him square. "I'm nursin' Victoria, takin' away the pain in her legs and gettin' her healthy."

"Following my instructions?" asks the doctor, his eyes stuck on the water and hot wraps.

"No," says Ma. "Doin' what works."

Victoria's pa's so mad, he's shakin'. "When did you stop doing what the doctor ordered?"

"Papa . . ." begins Victoria, but her pa shushes her with that look again.

"After we put Lizzy in the ground," I say, movin' to Ma's side.

Mr Cooper looks from me to Ma. "You've both been conspiring against my orders?" he asks.

I nod.

"Both of you gather your things," he says. "I'll get someone to take you back to the farm.".

Chapter 11
Victoria

Jacob's face drains of colour – of life – and he reaches for Mother Alice's shaking hand. I won't have them take the blame for me, for what I asked them to do.

"Papa," I say, "listen to me."

He takes no notice, but he can't make me be still, a quiet child, no brain of her own.

"Papa," I say, more firmly. "You have to listen."

"No, Victoria," Mother Alice says. "Leave it be. We can go."

The sorrow in her voice quickens my resolve, makes me determined. Victoria's a queen's name, a woman's name, Mother Alice's friend's name, my name. A name that gets things done.

I say, "Mother Alice knew, Papa. She knew how to take away the pain in my legs, stop the cramps, stop the agony."

"I told her …" says Papa, chin set, eyes dark storm clouds.

"To take care of me," I interrupt, grasping the warmth of Mother Alice's hand, enfolding it in mine. "To treat me as her own. And she did."

The doctor shakes his head. "There's nothing to be done for paralysis," he says, "only bracing the limbs up straight and tight."

"That's not so," I say, staring at my legs, at the wool wraps, now cool upon my skin. "Watch."

First, I wiggle my bare toes. I feel them rub against one another and touch the cold wooden rest upon the chair. My feet move next. They balance on my heels, then knock together, like hands clapping.

"See, Papa," I say.

His mouth drops, a mist of tears fills his eyes.

"Just one more thing," I say, lifting first my left leg, then my right. "They move. Both of my legs can move," I add, as if he can't see it for himself.

Papa drops down on his knees, wraps his arms around me in the chair. "Victoria, why have you all made this a secret? Kept me out?"

I think of the last month – him gone, hiding

away at the store – and say, "We haven't kept you out, Papa. You haven't let us in."

Papa wipes his hand across his eyes and asks, "How did this happen?"

I begin slowly, the story a patchwork quilt: red for anger, blue for hope, green for growth, yellow for joy and white for the sound of angels' wings. "At first, pain ate at me, filled me. The doctor's medicine was just tasteless candy that did nothing."

The doctor's young face crimsons while his eyes stay focused on his hands.

"Mother Alice nursed me as he said, while Jacob told me stories of those she'd healed before, and finally I asked if she could do something for me."

"And she did?" says Papa, clenching my hand tightly in his.

"Yes, she wrapped my legs in hot wool strips and for the first time in days the spasms stopped, the pain disappeared, and I could think again. I wanted to tell you, truly I did, but I knew I couldn't live if you made her stop and go back to the doctor's orders."

Papa says, "That's all?"

I shake my head. "Every day she wrung the cloths from steaming water, laid them on my legs, then stretched my muscles, pulling and prodding them back to shape. Her hands turned red, even blistered; she never once weakened, but nursed me day and night."

"And Jacob," says Papa. "What did he do?"

"He helped Mother Alice, but, even more, he makes me believe that I will run again, touch green grass with my toes, feel sunshine on my face."

"I haven't done that for you, have I?" asks Papa, his voice aching.

The doctor, shamefaced and wordless, drops down beside my feet, next to Papa, and runs a feather over my sole that makes me laugh.

Papa stands, turns to Mother Alice, takes her hand and says softly, "Thank you. Please forgive me for not trusting you to do what was best, to nurse her back to health."

"Never mind," says Mother Alice, her eyes on mine. "What matters is for Victoria to get well."

Once the doctor is done poking and prodding, making sure my paralysis is gone, he mutters something about meeting the banker and hastens out the door. Papa glances at Jacob, mutters, "I have to get back to the store," and follows.

Jacob, wordless, steps outside and disappears.

I've not yet done my exercises when Margaret whooshes through the front door, unruly red braids flying, freckled face full of laughter, and I'm caught up in the cyclone of her summer.

"Oh, Margaret, I've missed you so much," I say, throwing my arms around her, her crisp cotton dress crinkling beneath my fingertips. Soon, I will wear clothes, not a nightgown.

"You, too," she says, holding me back with tanned brown hands.

While she's grown taller, stronger, older, I've become a babe, and tears stream down my cheeks.

"It must have been dreadful," Margaret says, her blue eyes shining wet. "The infantile paralysis, losing Elizabeth and all."

Then we're both crying, hugging, missing all that's gone.

"Come, girls," says Mother Alice, bustling about the kitchen. "Lizzy would be makin' you both smile if she was here, so let's remember her the way she was. I made you buns for the homecoming."

Once the tea is poured, Mother Alice tries to slip away and hide in the garden, but I say, "Please stay," and so she does.

It's near supper when Margaret leaves, stepping backwards through the door. "You may not be running yet when school starts," she says, "but the boys will be chasin' after you when the term ends."

I laugh and call, "It's you the boys are after, so don't you go getting too tired to push my chair to class."

"If I'm pushin', you'll have to go where I want," she teases, waving from the bottom step. "And you never know where that will be!"

Her laughter leaves a trail of tinkling giggles behind. They fade, but the happiness stays, keeping time with my heart.

The door closes and there's just me, sitting at the table, and Mother Alice, standing at the stove, waiting for Papa and Jacob to come home.

I open *The Wonderful Wizard of Oz,* reread a piece – the *Magic Art of Humbug* – and wonder, if magic works, like Margaret's giggles, can it be humbug?

Was it magic that Scarecrow was happier

with a head stuffed with bran, pins and needles than with straw? That, even though the Wizard assured him he had no magic, he believed him when he said, *"Hereafter you will be a great man, for I have given you a lot of bran-new brains."*

What made Tin Woodman believe that a hole made by a tinsmith's shears, filled with a heart made entirely of silk and stuffed with sawdust, then soldered over with a patch, would be a very kind heart and bring him happiness?

And why did Cowardly Lion, after drinking everything from the Wizard's little green bottle, because *"Courage is always inside one"*, declare he felt *"Full of courage"*?

Can it really be that: *"It was easy to make the Scarecrow and the Lion and the Woodman happy, because they imagined the Wizard could do anything"*?

If that's all there is, perhaps if I can imagine my feet flying over the road, down the school halls, through the meadow, then I can run again.

While the sun slowly sinks, I keep reading ahead to keep my mind from Papa and from Jacob. Mother Alice slips outside into her garden to wait, and I'm alone with Dorothy, who, missing Kansas, decides it's time to go home.

Oz cuts silk strips of dark green, light green, emerald green, while Dorothy's needle flies back and forth, stitching them all together into a huge balloon, which Oz, slip-slap, paints with glue on the inside, to make it airtight.

As the balloon fills with hot air, it seems that Dorothy truly will get home, back to Kansas. I hold my breath, waiting for it to take flight, float through the sky.

But then, there's the Wizard of Oz, high in the basket, the balloon overhead tugging hard at the rope. He shouts, *"Come, Dorothy! Hurry up, or the balloon will fly away."*

I cannot breathe as Dorothy races after Toto, turns at last, dog in arms, to hear the crack as the balloon lets go. I see it climb, up, up, up into the sky, and drift away.

A tear escapes my eye and drips down my cheek, even though Oz is but a story, and I should have nothing to cry for any more – at least nothing that I can change.

The door opens and I close the book quickly, ashamed that I haven't waited to share this part with Jacob, as we shared the rest. But it is Papa stepping inside, his eyes smiling, not quite as they did before Elizabeth died, but not as empty as they've been.

My mouth is open, tongue still, like a bird's wings, spread the second before flight.

What should I say?

"Victoria," Papa says, shouldering his guilt. "I never realised before today that I'd given up one daughter while grieving for the other." He looks worn somehow, as if the weight of his grief has eaten away at his girth, made crevices in his round cheeks and splattered grey streaks in his thinning hair. "I'll try to do better."

"I miss her, too, and Mama," I say, "but they're together now … and we're here, with Mother Alice and Jacob."

The back door creaks and Mother Alice comes into the kitchen, bringing the earthy smell of soil clinging to her cheek, her fingers, her hands, her skirt. Her single word asks, "Hungry?" as if her caring is enough to make her happy.

Nobody mentions Jacob as we eat.

Dusk catches him when he comes home, his body barely a shadow – neither boy nor man – against the orange and yellow splashes of sunset that fill the western sky.

I think of Oz, of Dorothy trying to get home, even though Kansas is bleak and grey – is that how Jacob feels? That we're not home, just friends, like Scarecrow, Tin Woodman and Cowardly Lion?

Mother Alice sits in the rocker, chair squeaking while her hands fly. Purl two, knit two, purl two, knit two again.

Papa has the paper open, spread over the oil cloth but, instead of moving down the page, his eyes slide back and forth, to the parlour doors. I remember Mama's fingers at the piano, Lizzy pounding the keys, me singing, *"I once was lost, but now am found, was blind, but now I see,"* and Papa's deep voice blending in with it all. Perhaps memory will touch him, too, and bring him peace.

Jacob opens the door, bringing the cool night air with him as he steps inside. He says, "I can't work in the hardware store. I won't."

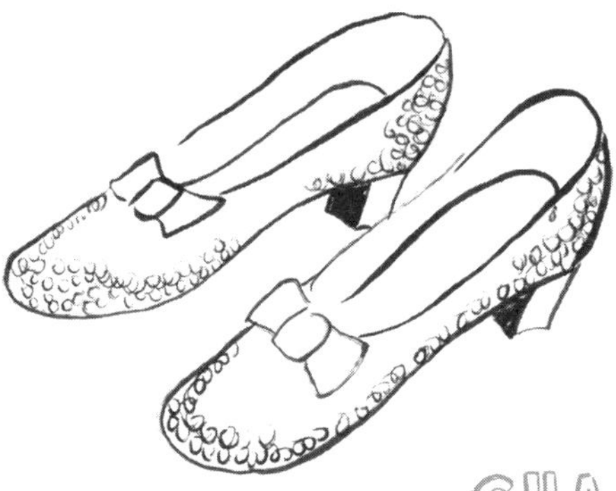

CHAPTER 12
JACOB

The electric lights are flickerin' on and off, like me, thinkin' I want to do this, then I want to do that.

Victoria's sittin' on the sofa, hands clamped on *The Wonderful Wizard of Oz.* I wonder if she's been waitin' for me to keep reading, or if she just went on ahead, found out if Dorothy gets home to Kansas.

Ma's click-clacking on her knitting needles – worryin' them to death, likely making big lumps in the brown sweater she's workin' on, thinkin' of a new way to convince me to stay on at the hardware store.

Mr Cooper, he's just staring down at the paper, like there's answers in other people's news.

It took me all afternoon thinkin', watchin' the stallion round up his little herd of mares and foals and countin' the half-grown baby rabbits ready to hop off on their own, to get me ready to tell them I can't do this no more.

I feel like the Wizard – everybody thinking I'm something I'm not – so I have to keep putting on different faces. When it turned out the Wizard was *"A little old man, with a bald head and a wrinkled face,"* I near fell off my chair. How must he have felt, all those years, buildin' masks to hide behind? I'd rather be a scarecrow with no brains, a tin woodman with no heart, or a lion that's afraid, than spend life worryin' about covering up a lie.

Ma must feel better, too, with everybody now knowing her nursing is fighting Victoria's infantile paralysis – helping her get strong.

I say again, louder, "I can't be a storekeeper," thinkin' it would have been better if Victoria had just told her pa right off how Ma's nursing made her feel better. People shouldn't be afraid of telling the truth.

Mr Cooper stands, nods at the table. "Eat, Jacob. We'll talk about this tomorrow. I think we all need to sleep on it."

Ma glances at him, takes one more quick

click-clack, then sets her knitting down. "Want your plate heated up, Jacob?"

I don't want to sleep on it.

"Ma, I want to talk now, not tomorrow," I say, my stomach growlin' as the smell of fried-up pork and apple sauce gets to my nose after she lifts the frypan lid that's been covering it.

"We'll do as Edward says and wait till mornin'," she says, quiet and firm-like.

I can be as stubborn as her, so waiting until mornin' won't make no difference in the end. I take the plate and say, "Cold pork is all right. So's morning."

"I'll make some tea," she says, reaching out to touch Mr Cooper's shoulder. "We're all needin' a cup."

Victoria says from the sofa, "Jacob, come listen while you eat. I'll read for a while, then you can read to the end. We're so close."

Plate in hand, I walk past Ma and Victoria's pa and drop down onto the soft chair opposite Victoria, who's bundled up in the quilt, same as usual, even though she doesn't have to hide her legs any longer.

I'm glad that Dr Oliver, thinking his book

learning was so much better than what Ma could do, knows now how Ma's nursing helped Victoria.

I can see Victoria has read ahead some in the book, but she turns back the pages and starts where we left off. I slip into Oz as fast as a rabbit down its hole, barely tasting Ma's supper and tea as I listen.

When my turn comes, I start reading out loud, not as good as Victoria, but not stumblin' over too many words. Ma listens a long while, then pats my arm and whispers, "Good night, Jacob. Call me when Victoria's ready for bed."

Her pa reaches down and hugs Victoria, then disappears behind Ma.

So Victoria and I go back to readin' about the travellers in Oz, who, all but Dorothy, are soon happy since they can do just what they please. I stop talking, stare outside at the stars sparkling and the full moon shining and the houses lying silent in the night, still wondering if I could do just what I pleased, what would it be.

"Victoria," I ask, my finger holdin' my place in Oz, "do you still want to be a teacher?"

She thinks for a minute. "Yes, everyone should

be able to journey to places like Oz, just using their imagination to take them. And they need to be able to read to do that."

"But what if your legs never got better – what if you never got out of the chair?"

She says slowly, "I can run along the yellow brick road with Scarecrow, Tin Woodman and Cowardly Lion, no matter where I am, even in the chair." Her eyes twinkle like the stars. "But I'm determined to walk and to run, even if I have to use a cane to help me do it." She kicks the quilt off her legs. "See, my feet are running already."

And they are.

She's quiet for a minute, then she asks, "If you don't want to be a storekeeper, what do you want to be, Jacob?" Her eyes are on her feet, not looking at me. "Go back and be a farmer?"

"Maybe," I say slowly, not so sure of anything any more.

I start reading again – where Scarecrow has a new idea. *"'Why not call the Winged Monkeys, and ask them to carry you over the desert?'"*

By now I'm readin' fast. The end of the book is so close, and I'm half afraid Dorothy won't get home across the desert to Kansas at all. And I'm half afraid she will, but find out her Aunt Em and Uncle Henry got blown away in the cyclone, too, and maybe died, like Pa, so there's no going back to what she had before. If she does get to Kansas and they're gone, her friends will be left behind in Oz, so she won't even have them any more.

What would *I* do? Keep looking for a way back to Kansas or stay in Oz?

But even calling on the Winged Monkeys doesn't get Dorothy home, so the four friends get started on one last try to find Glinda, the most powerful of all the witches, who rules over the Quadlings, and whose castle stands on the edge of the desert, to see if she can help.

"Shall I read for a while?" Victoria asks. "Your voice must be tired."

It is, but it seems important to find out the end of the story tonight, before I talk to Ma and Victoria's pa in the morning. I hand her the book.

Getting to Glinda isn't easy. First they come to a forest where, *"There was no way of going around it, for it seemed to extend to the right and left as far as they could see; and, besides, they did not dare change the direction of their journey for fear of getting lost*." Scarecrow tries, but it's Tin Woodman and his axe who get them through.

Soon I'm hunched on the edge of the chair, seein' the country made entirely of china in the illustrations, with tiny houses that only reach to Dorothy's waist and people no higher than her knee. I imagine them, the travellers walkin' through this land, and the china things gettin' broken, even without bein' stepped on.

Victoria stops reading. "What do you think it would be like to be so much bigger than everything else?"

"I shouldn't like being careful of little things all the time," I say, thinkin' about the hardware store and how hard it's been these past months, trying to get everything just right, to make Ma happy. Maybe if I'd been aimin' to please myself, things would have been different.

"Me neither," she says. "Nor would I want to be made of china and break so easy, even if I could be mended every time."

While she reads the next part, I wonder if you're ever really whole again, once you've been broke bad once and mended, like Victoria from the paralysis. Even if she looks the same on the outside, surely she'll be different on the inside.

When we get to the part where Cowardly Lion's tail smashes the china church to bits, I think about how easy it is for things not to turn out like you plan. Lion was only jumping to escape by the wall, not meaning to hurt anything at all.

I'm guessin' maybe things at the hardware store aren't what Mr Cooper thought they'd be neither. There's all the times I snuck out through the back and ran up to the meadow – spent my time with the horses and didn't do any work at all. I wonder if he knows?

The next country the travellers come to in Oz is full of long grass and muddy holes, kind of like when it's been raining for days and days at the farm. Strange to think how Cowardly Lion believes it's perfect and Scarecrow finds it gloomy – a bit like me and Mr Cooper, seeing the hardware in different ways.

And here, Lion saves all the other animals from a giant spider. Even though he was happy before, Lion promises he will come back to rule over them as soon as Dorothy is safely on her way – for that's what lions do – be king of all the beasts.

But still there's no Glinda and no land of the Quadlings. Instead, Dorothy must summon the Winged Monkeys for help one last time, to fly them over the people with shooting heads who won't let the travellers pass across their hill. I stare at the picture, thinking how real it all seems, like a photograph, not a made-up drawing.

I put my hand over my mouth, trying to stop a yawn. "How many pages left?" I ask, just as the electric lights blink off. I grab the lantern that Ma starts each night at dark, in case the lights go out.

"Just five more," says Victoria, counting as she flicks them over. "It must be your turn to read again."

"It'll be slower," I say.

"That's all right," says Victoria. "I don't mind. You have a good voice, and you hardly miss any words at all any more."

"I don't, do I?" I say, feelin' more pride than when I ploughed my first field with the Clydesdale horses.

I take the book, careful to keep her place.

It's at Chapter 23, called, *Glinda The Good Witch Grants Dorothy's Wish.* The end comes quick. Dorothy gives the Golden Cap to Glinda, who uses its three commands to have the monkeys take Scarecrow, Tin Woodman, and Cowardly Lion to where they want to be.

Finally, Glinda tells Dorothy, *"Your Silver Shoes will carry you over the desert. If you had known their power you could have gone back to your Aunt Em the very first day you came to this country."*

I drop the book for a moment and ask, "Victoria, if you were Dorothy, would you have wanted that – to miss making friends and helping them get what they most desired?"

"Not for a minute," she says quickly. "Not even to get home."

"Me neither," I say, thinkin' that, if Ma hadn't married Victoria's pa, I'd have missed out on havin' sisters, especially little Lizzy, even though she died from the infantile paralysis. We wouldn't have been here for Ma to nurse Victoria, and she could have ended up in a wheelchair forever.

When I start readin' again, Dorothy clicks the heels of her silver shoes together three times and goes off whirling through the air. She lands in Kansas, rolling over and over on the grass, to find Aunt Em and Uncle Henry didn't get blown away in the cyclone, just the house that killed the Wicked Witch to get Dorothy the silver shoes in the first place. Things are different, but Dorothy is finally home … like me.

Victoria whispers, "Thank you for giving me this book and reading it to me each night. Without Dorothy, Scarecrow, Tin Woodman and Cowardly Lion, I might never have got better at all."

"I was glad to do it," I say, remembering the day I bought it. "Without Oz, I would still be doing letters, not reading a real book."

I'm not sure what else to say, so I just go, knock on Ma's door for her to help Victoria to bed and climb up the ladder to my room in the garret.

The moonlight through the one tiny window is bright enough to see by as I drop my clothes and crawl under the quilt on my pallet. I lie there, eyes wide open, wishin' I could whirl away to Oz and have adventures of my own.

Then I think what I've found in just one book,

and about all the others there are to read if I was back in school. There must be some way for me to go again, if I ask Victoria's pa to help. Maybe there's more stories like Oz, or maybe I could get more learning, like the doctor had, to add to what Ma's already showed me about nursin' sick animals and people.

As my eyes get heavy, this afternoon fills my head – Mr Higgins' stallion racing through the meadow, fence penning him in, while I'm running free, wherever I want.